Tour
Book

RACHEL PFENNIG HALES

Published 2021 by Your Book Angel
Copyright © Rachel Pfennig Hales

All rights reserved. No part of this book may be reproduced, stored, or transmitted by any means—whether auditory, graphic, mechanical, or electronic—without written permission of both publisher and author, except in the case of brief excerpts used in critical articles and reviews. Unauthorized reproduction of any part of this work is illegal and is punishable by law.

The characters are all mine, any similarities with other fictional or real persons/places are coincidental.

Printed in the United States
Edited by Keidi Keating
Layout by Rochelle Mensidor

ISBN: 978-1-7356648-4-2

To the man who made the road feel like home,
who read this book at every stage,
and who always has my back.
Thank you for sharing this with me.

TABLE OF CONTENTS

Author's Note vii
PROLOGUE: **Show Time** ix
CHAPTER ONE: **21 Hours Until Show Time** 1
CHAPTER TWO: **15 Hours Until Show Time** 7
CHAPTER THREE: **13 Hours Until Show Time** 21
CHAPTER FOUR: **11 Hours Until Show Time** 38
CHAPTER FIVE: **10 Hours Until Show Time** 50
CHAPTER SIX: **9 Hours Until Show Time** 66
CHAPTER SEVEN: **8 Hours Until Show Time** 72
CHAPTER EIGHT: **7 Hours Until Show Time** 83
CHAPTER NINE: **6 Hours Until Show Time** 95
CHAPTER TEN: **5 Hours Until Show Time** 101
CHAPTER ELEVEN: **4 Hours Until Show Time** 116
CHAPTER TWELVE: **3 Hours Until Show Time** ... 130
CHAPTER THIRTEEN: **2 Hours Until Show Time** 137
CHAPTER FOURTEEN: **30 Minutes Until Show Time** 146
CHAPTER FIFTEEN: **Encore** 152
Acknowledgments 159

AUTHOR'S NOTE

This is my community. These are my friends. This is my workplace, and at times, has been my address. Concert touring asks us to be flexible, smart, and quick on our feet. We have to be easy-going yet full speed, all at once. It has been ten years since I put on my first tour credential and was welcomed backstage. This book strives to show a glimpse of this quiet yet fierce society, as I have experienced it.

This is not a book about rock stars. This is not a book about tabloid tales, or even about a single tour. Dozens of touring professionals, from several different tours have been interviewed throughout this project. These roadies shared moments from their standard show days, technical jobs, and extensive careers.

Very few names have been changed; however, upon request some have, along with key identifiers, to guard the privacy of these individuals.

The "Show Day" depicted here aims to represent an average day backstage at an arena production, as described by the live event technicians who contributed. Life on tour is unpredictable, and the industry evolving. This book hopes to introduce and recognize the invisible teams behind today's favorite concert tours, and to celebrate an industry that builds iconic rock and roll moments every day.

PROLOGUE

SHOW TIME

House lights drop, and a collective cheer grows. The darkness swells in anticipation. Hundreds of cell phones glow, replacing traditional lighters, flickering off the faces of the crowd. Hairs stand on end. Adrenaline pumps. A whistle. A hoot. Someone yells, "Freebird!"

A breath of silence.

That first chord screams from the speakers and across the swarming arena. On cue, the lights flash to flood the stage, radiating in pinks and purples and whites. The audience lurches and sways as the concert commands.

I'm here for a song, maybe two. I am off to the side, backstage right or left, maybe sitting on a short road case behind the barricade line. Never out with the audience. Most of the road crew won't venture out there unless a job or an emergency requires it. Or, maybe, for a really hot groupie.

The music is loud, but not overwhelming. In the wings, backup singers wait their turn. A small group of carpenters brace a large prop on the ramp, ready to roll it into place. The video screens, taller than the stage is wide, dance with the beat.

There is not a great view of the artist from here. A lot of shoulder and back. A lot of hair shakes. Everyone on stage has their own routine. Walk here, almost run there. Jump a little. Point to a pretty girl near the front, preferably one with a boyfriend. Jealousy always plays well on the large video screens. Gesture at her. Wink. Walk backward toward the other side of the stage. The guy on spotlight knows just where the star is, and plans to be. The spotlight guy has his own show routine, too, of course.

Each prop, each cool trick, every costume or scene change requires the hidden help of someone behind the stage, someone under the stage, or someone in the ceiling. Every department has its own gear, its own elements to control, but each piece must come together as if one person is creating the whole experience.

A few guys help a dancer into a toaster lift that will shoot up through the stage, popping her out on cue. Two more run the fly gag from the rafters, sending spectacles soaring over the crowd. Camera close-ups for the first song, the third, the beginning of the fourth, to start. Help with a costume change stage right. Be ready with a prop, an instrument, an extra flashlight on the stairs at the same time, for every performance. Everyone has their own cues to run, and they expect everyone else to hit theirs, too. Blocked. Rehearsed. Consistent. This is our show.

I spend my time between cues watching the audience. Thousands of people watching us, only seeing what's up on stage. At least, that's the goal. They are here to see a concert, the name on the ticket stub and the T-shirts. They've come from who knows where, doing who knows what all day. A group of girlfriends dance and sing along, while the bachelors behind them try to join in. Maybe she's a new mom on her first night out since baby, just trying to feel like herself again. Maybe he got a promotion, or she just lost her job. Maybe their band will make it big one day, too.

They listen to the music at parties and at work. They know all the words and belt them loud in their cars. They have the artist's pictures on posters and follow all the magazine stories. They imagine what life might be like if they were rock stars. Or, could at least meet one in person.

They jump and wiggle with the beat. They shout, reaching for the stage. They hold signs. They sing along. They each came here separately from different worlds, but in the dark, with the music loud and engulfing, all that disappears. When they cheer, they cheer together. When it's quiet, they are quiet together. And when that all-time favorite is finally played, they sing with one voice.

It doesn't matter who knows the words and who doesn't. The crowd does. It doesn't matter who can actually hit the belt note at the end. The crowd can. Together, they take on a new form. Every few songs the lights pass over a section of the audience, highlighting certain bodies, but never breaking their unity. For this one song, this one concert, this one night, they are one-and they are always singing.

We are there too, in the dark under the show, behind it, and above it. Running it. Our job is to put on a really kickass concert. Our job is to make it look easy. We have to be so good at what we do, no one knows we're doing it. Together, we have to be safe and smart. Together, we have to be flawless, so the audience can keep rocking.

In a few hours, the crowd will have gone home to their beds. The stars might be appearing at an after party, or finishing interviews. We will be tearing it all down. We will pack up the gear. We will load up more than a dozen tractor trailers. We will shower and climb on the tour buses where we sleep. It will be after midnight when we finally clamber aboard our rolling home, crawl into our bunks, and head out to the next city. Tomorrow, we will build the production again. We'll greet another audience. Then, we'll pack it back on the trucks. That's the job. That's life on tour.

CHAPTER ONE

21 HOURS UNTIL SHOW TIME

LOAD-OUT

*D*on't *fucking touch that! You. Yeah, you!*
 Beep. Beep. Beep. Watch out for the forklift. The dollies. The trucks. The truss. The chains.

Clink. Clink. Clang. Cling. Clang.

You! Go with him.

You! Push that cart stage left. Look for the guy with the green mohawk.

Move. Move. MOVE. Don't hesitate. Don't slow down. Show is over, and we have to go, go. GO. Stop for a minute and get run over. Do your job. Listen to directions. Go. Go. Get out of the way.

Okay, everyone with me. We need four people on that side. Three more and me over here. Ready to lift? One. Two.

Metal against metal. Wheels scrape concrete. Look both ways. Chalk-sketched marks on the floor. Wrenches and hammers and cables and screws and casters and pickles. Remotes and ladders and deck legs and road cases.

Clunk. Clunk, clunk. Clunk.

I need hands over here.

Speakers and lights and video screens are lowered to the floor from their show positions. Gear breaks down and packs into protective, rolling black cases. They swivel across arena floors. They push up onto truck beds.

Paper schedules get torn off walls. Done. Show is over, concert is finished, people are out. Brooms push old cups and chewed gum and confetti. Gear is gone, things pack up, off we go. Time for everyone to get moving.

Shower. Food. How long is tonight's drive?

Where's the food?

Pizza again?

Pizza again!

Finish up fast.

Drivers get ready.

Load up, load out.

ROADIE RULES

I can pick the roadies out of any crowd.

A small army, surrounded by a sea of civilians, we tend to dress in uniform. Faces will be tired, maybe unshowered, and most likely wearing either a "Fuck Off" or "Fuck Yeah" defiance.

Wear all black, always. That's basic. We need to blend in, unseen backstage.

Closed-toed shoes, preferably steel-toed boots. Cargo shorts or utility belt, even on nights off. Some will be missing chunks of fingers. Others may be missing full fingers. One I know will be missing an ear.

Tattoos are a plus, worn as badges of honor, as are beards, mohawks, piercings and shaved heads. When in doubt, asking about these artistic identifiers always gets us talking.

We walk in like we are taking over, and usually do. Our laminated backstage passes—discreet, yet purposefully visible to any who bother to look—grant us VIP access almost anywhere, including private clubs, closed liquor stores, and most likely, your hotel room, if we ask.

We are not groupies. We are not fans. We are with the show. We are touring live entertainment technicians. We are roadies.

If you go without pissing people off, you can stay. But out here, it is more than a job. It is a lifestyle. Like any community, there are certain rules you have to follow. Call it a pirate's code, to self-govern the chaos.

Some rules we're told. Straightforward, and essential.

First of all, keep it to yourself. All of it, always. No pictures, no autographs, no talking about anything you see. Amidst rock stars and red carpets, excitement is reserved for the outer circle. We are the inner. Or, at least inner adjacent.

Your cell phone should be considered a vital life source and is to never leave your reach. On show days, the same goes for your radio. If you don't answer on the first call, people will automatically assume you've fallen into a dumpster or been kidnapped by super-fans. They will send out a search party, or at least, call you incessantly until you do answer. You could always report back with "10-100," which announces to anyone listening that you're on the toilet, but given the choice, I'd opt for the search party.

Don't drink the bus water.

Though the privacy is tempting, don't use the artists' bathroom, even before they're in.

If it has a manager's signature, any receipt is fair game: outrageously-priced champagne, inflatable prop cell phones, didgeridoos for hip-hop groups. People buy some weird crap in the name of show biz. Trust me, it's better not to ask.

If you're not early, you're late.

Hustle and do your job. Second chances aren't guaranteed. There will not be a third chance. This world is not for everyone, and others will let you know if it's not working out. The show has to come first. You have to be there for your crew.

Other rules take time to learn. Like, only pack what you're willing to carry. Or, that words like "per diem," "road rate," and "retainer" are beautiful things.

Laundry gets sent out every two weeks, but no one is paying attention to what you're wearing. Is it comfortable? Can you work in it? Do you have extra socks?

Some venue showers are even too gross for shower shoes, so sometimes, the best option is just to go without. Non-show days bring hotel rooms ranging from Holiday Inn to Ritz-Carlton. A good hotel room is marked by the bathroom, unless of course, there's a balcony.

At hotels, in fear of nothing in particular, only answer to the Roadie Knock. Side note: never show, share or discuss the Roadie Knock. If you don't already know it, you probably won't.

One the tour bus: no talking in the bunks, no loud alarms, no solid waste, no messing with the thermostat.

There are twelve bunks, but avoid twelve on a bus whenever possible. If you miss call time, expect the bus to "oil spot"—or, leave without you. If you do run late, it's smart to make friends with the driver. He might stall.

Second dinner—or after-show food—will be provided, but don't bitch if it's pizza a few nights in a row. Sometimes there is just no other choice at 11:30 p.m. in the middle of nowhere.

Driving into a day off, expect a party. Drinking in the front, smoking in the back; though cigarettes are rarely allowed anymore. Keep the sleep bay quiet. No booty calls on the bus. Again, no solid wastes. And, seriously, don't pass out in either the front or back lounge. Those are social spaces, and others will not be held responsible for what they draw on you.

The truth is, a lot of our rules are only rules because, at some point, somewhere, some idiot required us to make a rule. It seems some people need to be told not to pee on the arena floor, not to wash their clothes in bus water, or that Vicodin smoothies are a bad idea.

Life on tour— a different city every day, calling a bus home—it's a vacuum. A time capsule. Nothing else exists. Family, houses, pets—they are all a world away. The tour is our work life, our social life, our private life, for now. We have rules to keep the group balanced. To look out for each other. And because, after a show, really, most of us just want a beer, a piece of pizza, and to go to bed.

BUS DRIVER

The caravan of tour buses cruises three miles over the speed limit across quiet interstates. They don't always travel together. On long drives each bus leaves as its department is ready, but on a short run between cities, everyone waits to roll as a group. Inside, the touring road crew sleeps. We are tucked into bunks as drivers steer through tunnels and across bridges, around cities and past states. Our driver slept all day, preparing to drive through the night. He takes it seriously. He knows everyone on his bus has their lives in his hands. Plus the bus behind his. And the bus behind that. He keeps the vehicle clean, his fluids down and his driving music low. As everyone rests, the crew is his responsibility. Tomorrow's show won't wait.

CHAPTER TWO

15 HOURS UNTIL SHOW TIME

ROAD STORY

"We had this huge harvest and went over to the race track to smoke it. We were always smoking pot out there. It was right by our house and no one ever seemed to care or notice what we did. We had this new weed and some guy walking by smells it. He comes over. We were sort of freaking out, you know? My friend wanted to run, but I was young and arrogant.

"Turns out he was cool, just looking to buy. Actually, he turns out to be the bassist for the band playing that night. We shared what we had, and he gave us passes to the show. I had never been to a concert before. I was a little punk, so, of course, I wanted to see what those 'All Access' passes could do. I went backstage. No problem.

"It was chaos. I had no idea what was going on. There were people everywhere. We were just in the way. Then this guy who was yelling at everyone, turned and started yelling at us. He said if we were going to hang around, we better start helping load the trucks with gear. He promised $35 and a T-shirt. That was my first load-out. I can't even guess how many I've done by now."

Rigger, sometimes a carpenter, forty-eight years old

WAKING UP

I feel the buzz of my alarm before I hear it. The vibration starts slow and soft, gradually growing both stronger and louder. It doesn't matter. I will silence it altogether before anyone else can hear it.

It is dark as I snooze the alarm. I try to avoid looking at the screen so my eyes will stay adjusted to the limited light in our sleep area. I know it reads 5:36 a.m. My body is tired, but my mind is already churning. I doubt it ever really stopped in the four hours since I curled up to sleep, but that's the pace on tour.

There are eight other people sleeping either below, next to, or behind me. I always try to claim the top, front, driver's-side bunk in the bus. There are usually six beds on each the left and right hand sides, stacked three tall in the middle of the bus, separated by a narrow hallway. Twelve people makes for a crowded ride, so the ideal range is seven to ten, leaving a couple of bunks open for overnight bags. At least in the United States.

I used to sleep on the top right, in the back row of bunks. Only a thin wall separated my head from the TV mounted in the corner of the lounge, and all night long, I could hear whatever was happening back there. Steady, thumping bass, violent video games, porn. It didn't take long to decide the front bunks were more my style. Some people prefer the bottom, but I don't mind climbing the other beds like a ladder to reach my nook up high. Once I'm up there, I am alone.

The bunk is about eight feet long and three feet wide. For some of the bigger members of the crew, sleeping can be cramped and uncomfortable. At five-foot-six-inches, though, I have just enough space to store a change of clothes and a makeup bag at my feet, while still stretching out comfortably. Truth is, I love it up here. It is always cold, mostly to keep germs at bay, so I am wrapped up in at least one big comforter. I am also wearing fuzzy socks, a fleece, and an oversized sweatshirt, hood up. I fell asleep with my retainers and ear buds in, sleep mask on. A book is tucked somewhere, for long rides, but I usually only make it through a few paragraphs before retreating into sleep again. With the thin curtain pulled tight, it feels like a cocoon, rocking calmly with the motions of the bus. My own little sliver of space to recharge.

The phone gently stirs again, plugged into the outlet at my head and tucked under my pillow. My sleep mask has slipped off at some point during the night, and my eyes blink open to the dark confines of the bunk. Hitting silence without looking, I know I will not be going back to sleep. I snuggle in the warmth of my blankets for a minute, thinking through the day: What city are we in? What did I advance with the catering team for breakfast? Please let them have coffee up and waiting when we walk in, like I asked, or I will be hearing about it all day.

Outside my curtain, a few other alarms start to sound. Some, loud and abrasive, send chills down my spine. As part of the main production team, I am always in the first wave of people into the building. Some others on the bus might have thirty or forty minutes before they have to get to work, and like me, will wait as long as possible before getting up.

But, now it is time to start my day. I work as production assistant or production coordinator or something involving hospitality for the artists—my role changes depending on the tour. A lot of people are needed to build a concert and, usually, I am involved in organizing all those people. Flights, hotel rooms, food. Our team arrives early to assign the various rooms as offices, dressing rooms, shower rooms and more. I need to check on breakfast. We need to make sure the trucks are here for load-in. The production manager will be ready to leave in twelve minutes, and I want to be waiting. I switch on the small reading light set into the wall near my head. It's time to wake up.

Someone else is crawling out of his bed, probably the stage manager. He will head into the arena with us. He sleeps on the bottom, back left, and literally rolls off his mattress onto the floor. Like most, he sleeps in boxers, and maybe a T-shirt. Standing in the small aisle between the beds, he will pull on the same dark cargo shorts from yesterday and a fresh, black shirt (probably a freebie, labeled with the logo of another band or vendor he's worked for.) Grabbing steel-toed boots and a clean pair of socks, he heads to the front lounge. He's ready.

I prefer to get dressed inside my bunk. It's not ideal, but I like the privacy. Before falling asleep last night, I piled a new shirt, clean underwear and socks, my jeans and bra in the back corner by my feet. Still under the covers this morning, I pull off my sweatpants and throw them to the foot of the bed. Using my best yoga-bridge pose, the bottoms slide on easy enough. I can sit up at an angle, propped against the wall at my head, so changing my shirt is not a problem either. I'll put on my socks once I climb down.

Sitting up as much as possible, I take care of my limited morning beauty routine. I wiped with cleanser last night at the venue, so my face is as clean as it will be. Contacts in, unless it's the third or forth show in a row, then glasses will have to do. Light concealer, though I know it really doesn't do much to hide the circles permanently resting under my eyes. Nude-colored eyeshadow also helps. Two quick swipes of blush on each cheekbone. ChapStick. Mascara. If I wake up in a hotel, I try leaving my hair down, otherwise it's pulled back into a ponytail. If I wake up late on the bus, I'll skip right to the mascara. If it's really late, I'll shove the mascara in my jeans pocket and apply it late in the morning, if at all.

I've never worn much makeup. The routine wouldn't really be different if I were at home, though the lighting would be better. Mornings have always been slow for me and taking time to wake up, when I can, helps ease the transition into my day. On the road, I think the ritual is more for my mental state than my physical. A little something to help me feel like myself. A routine. Waking up every morning, the dab of blush and swipe of mascara reminds me I am in control. I am still *me*.

As I finally slide out of my bunk, climbing down by placing my toes on the edge of the middle bunk on my way, I already know it will be a long day. Someone is complaining to the bus driver about last night's bumpy ride, and the production manager's alarm is still going off.

It is the start of another day.

I zip my pants, and straighten myself in the dark hall. I grab my socks from the bunk, then draw the curtain closed. My purse, still packed from last night, is waiting in a spare bunk. My shoes sit lined up with others along the baseboard. When possible, I wait to use the bathroom and brush my teeth until we get into the building.

We left an arena last night, miles away, walking through a dark parking lot and onto the bus we call home. We slept while drivers carried us along major highways and back roads, through cities and states. Soon, we will be stepping down off the bus, walking across a different dark parking lot, and into another, different venue. Where we are doesn't matter much. Neither does the day of the week. On tour, there are only two days in any week: it is either a show day, or a non-show day. And today is a show day.

WHAT YOU WON'T HEAR

Everyone wants to hear the crazy stories. They want to hear about the celebrities, their flaws and their weird, fabulous quirks. They want to know about drugs and sex, and surprisingly little about rock and roll. They want to hear about the late nights, the VIP parties, the swag. Maybe they'll listen to accounts of long hours and grueling conditions. Maybe they'll ask about the technology. But really, they want to hear the tabloid version of backstage.

That part does exist, of course.

I once saw Tom Cruise sing karaoke at some afterparty in Malaysia, and then again in Vancouver. I've helped Santana move a couch and babysat Slash's kid during a show. I've toasted with Dom Perignon, even though I couldn't pronounce it. Once—and only once—I walked into a hotel room and saw a literal mound of cocaine.

I've been to the Grammys twice, as well as the American Music Awards, and stood in the back parking lot at something for MTV. Admittedly, I've always used the stage door and never once walked a red carpet. I stood on the field at the World Cup in South Africa. I've rocked out with Ryan Seacrest for New Year's. I've flown charter. I've missed a few commercial flights. I have visited five of the seven continents, and in 2010, I ran out of passport pages.

I've worked shows at Madison Square Garden, the United Center, the Staples Center, the Grand Ole Opry, and the O2 arenas in London, Berlin, and Dublin. I've worked four shows in old Italian castles and one at a Target.

My longest stretch is fifty-two hours awake, with only a few stolen moments of "sleep" on the van rides between shows. I've played empty, muddy fields, with no cell service or Internet. I've been tipped by pop stars in perfume and smart electronics. I sat at the top of the upgrade list for a number of five-star hotels. I confronted a thief in Spain and talked my way onto an active airport runway in Mexico City. I've been to countless motorcycle rallies, playing to older, topless crowds. I've been escorted by an entourage of Hells Angels. I have taken three severed fingers to the ER. I've been screamed at in public. Once, I swear, I was almost struck by lightning.

I've been excited. I've been scared. I have been behind that velvet rope. I've cried and bitched and lost my temper. I've been walked on and taken advantage of. I'm sure I've done the same to others. I've met hookers, strippers, and racecar drivers; clowns and philanthropists; vintners and rock legends; lots of runners, border patrol officers, auditing agents, cowboys, translators and alcoholics, both recovering and indulging.

By now, I've been backstage at well over one hundred concerts.

I've been allowed to press the button that sends pyrotechnics shooting through the air. I've soared in a fly gag, usually reserved for pop stars to glide through the air. I tried my hand at calling shots for the video crew, and understood right away, I wasn't that good. I've been up on stage, and watched in awe with the audience.

Concerts are supposed to be fun. They are supposed to look effortless. The lifestyle adds to that allure. The gossip helps distract from the work of the show. The real story is much quieter. It is hidden, camouflaged between spotlight beams. It lives and moves, unnoticed.

Life backstage has a lot more personality than the tabloids, or any book, could ever capture. Sure, there are stories I tell, but there are still stories I don't (and not just because I've signed a career's worth of non-disclosures).

WHAT'S IN A NAME?

Some people don't like the word "roadie." Like it's some kind of insult. An antiquated term, glorifying wild nights and reckless binges that no longer represent the industry. They would rather hear "touring professional." Maybe it's "stagehand", or "electrician" or "carpenter" or "engineer." Just plain "crew" might do, or "technician." "Production", "C Party", "delinquents", "guys" , "hey you", "fucking assface"... there a lot of things we could be called.

To many, though, the word "roadie" is a badge of honor, secured with the credential through long hours and hard work. There is pride in generations of pirates, renegades and rebels, living on the road, building big shows. Being called a "roadie" is earned, and important title that stands for history and strength. To be a roadie is to join a lifestyle, a community, a family.

PRODUCTION MANAGER

Opie is one of the first to arrive every morning. As production manager, he gets the day, the show, and the work started. Before semi-trailer doors open to unload any gear, before several dozen local stage hands join a few dozen touring technicians to build a show, while forklifts still sit empty, coffee is being brewed, and most of the crew is still on the bus, the PM is already in the arena.

His eyes squeeze tight, but not fast enough. The bus was dim, and the hazy blue of the morning parking lot walk gentle, but the harsh fluorescent wash of the loading dock stings. It takes effort to open his eyes to the bright inside lights. Opie forces one eyelid open, then the next. Already, the air is a mix of bacon and gasoline. Instead of chasing breakfast, the production manager—or PM—heads straight to the arena floor.

Known to most everyone as "Opie," Dale is soft spoken. Not meek by any means, but reserved. Calculating. Humble, even. As production manager, his job is to supervise the technical needs for the show, lead the crew, and advance the tour. Every detail of how the show connects can be traced back to him. He has subtle, reddish hair and a thin frame. Unlike most road veterans, Opie actually looks younger than he is, easily passing for forty-something. Like most days, he is wearing jeans and a T-shirt, with a zip-up hoodie from some other tour he's done.

The path from the back docks to the main space is a tunnel, crossing from the soon-to-be high-traffic hallway backstage, under the seats, and out into a large, oval arena. The cement is gray and cold. Dull-colored chairs push up from the flat, open floor practically reaching the ceiling. Last night, they were probably full of fans watching a basketball game or a hockey game or some other show. It will be packed again tonight. When the artists enter, this space will be crammed full of waiting fans. The stage will be set, the instruments tuned and the crew ready. It will be loud and dark and carry the full stress of a live show.

Opie knows that tens-of-thousands of people have spent hundreds-of-thousands of dollars to be part of the audience tonight. The promoter has fronted money to make the show happen. The building needs to be paid, and so do the local labor offices, the road crew, and the vendors. Thousands of people rely on the success of this show—of last night's and tomorrow's. Every performance matters. Every night it has to happen right. It has to be spectacular.

Opie is responsible for making sure all that happens. Stopping under the large archway at the edge of the empty room, he is the first one here. He shoves his hands deep into the pockets of his sweatshirt. Not many people ever see the arena like this. It is still. Quiet, except for the gentle hum of the idling trailers out back.

"I just don't want to fuck it up," he offers, sincerely. "I worry about it all the time."

With over thirty years in touring rock and roll, Opie has worked with the best, from AC/DC to The Rolling Stones, Black Sabbath, Guns 'N Roses, Metallica, solo Ozzy, Def Leppard, and a few others he never remembers to add. Opie's résumé reads like a "Who's Who" of rock and roll. He was one of the first, and is one of the greats, though he'd never say that.

"It all just sort of happened," he says of starting out. "A lot of being in the right place at the right time. A lot of people trusting me, giving me a chance. Plus, back when I started, things were so different."

Opie grew up alongside the industry. His first tour was with Sha Na Na in 1981 while he was still a teenager, before there were strict job titles or specific departments. "There were only a handful of us on the crew, and everything had to get done. The job was to make sure there was a show, whatever that meant. Hanging drapes in the dressing room, building the stage, setting up instruments, maybe focusing some lights. Everyone pitched in where they could. We just got stuff done."

That's still the job, really. At the end of the day, whatever title a person holds, whatever the department is called, whoever is in charge of what, stuff still has to get done. The audience is on their way, and start time does not change. The show has to be ready. It has to be right.

Opie's current crew has ten different technical departments: audio, automation, backline, carpentry, dressing rooms/hospitality, lighting, pyrotechnics, rigging, video, plus a production team to coordinate all the technical crew's needs. There's also a tour manager who runs all broader show and artists' needs, truck drivers and bus drivers, a merchandising rep selling band gear to fans, a person setting up VIP parties for high-end tickets, security, and a promoter representative from the company paying for everything. A lot more goes into shows now. A concert is not just about the music and the fans anymore. These events have grown into full sensory experiences, with elaborate elements and complex technology.

This early in the morning, though, it's hard to imagine anything will happen here tonight. Every bolt and screw and cable that creates the concert is still waiting on the truck. Right now, the arena is just a concrete room.

"I do love building a show each day, getting it ready," Opie walks out into the vast, seemingly boundless bowl. "The pressure is on. The machine is moving. It's fun. But there has to be a solid foundation first, before the tour even starts."

It all starts with a design. Show designers and artists provide a concept, or picture, to build toward. Production then figures out how the concept becomes reality, and stays on budget. Opie coordinates with vendors to create all the tangible elements of the show, physically translating that picture to an audience. He collects all the different vendors who loan and supply various aspects, like gear and resources and people. Together, they build the tour.

Opie smiles to himself. The prep part is his favorite. "It's consuming, but sort of exhilarating to watch the idea grow into reality. I've done a little bit of everything, so I am able to understand the scope of work for each department. Productions have grown so much over the years. Someone had to be in charge of bringing it all together. I was here, so I did it."

He pauses.

This is the last time the arena will be quiet until after the show. Opie will be one of the last out of the building tonight, too. From now until then, there will be work to do. His voice softens as he continues, "The trick is understanding it's not about what any one person wants. It's about what is best for the whole.

"I'm proud of what we will build here. Of course, a show is only as good as the crew that creates it. The biggest part of my gig is supporting them." A faint beeping starts from outside, where a truck is backing into place. A bus-load of crew enter at the dock door, looking for coffee. The day is starting.

"I try to remember to enjoy this moment, before it all happens. All of this is more than a career. It's my life. I'm really lucky, but, there is no telling when it will end." He looks up to the grid in the ceiling, some eighty feet above his head, then down to his shoes. "The bands I work with are getting older. So am I. That's just fact.

"The most important thing I've learned? We are all replaceable. Every one of us. Even me. Even the artist, in most ways. If I step away, someone will be there to replace me. Quick and easy as that." Opie smiles again, shaking his head. "It's actually reassuring. The show will always go on."

CHAPTER THREE

13 HOURS UNTIL SHOW TIME

A BRIEF HISTORY OF TOURING ROCK AND ROLL

First-generation roadies, the senior organizers of shows still today, all have the same sort of story: a friend's cousin, or someone, had a band that was pretty good. He—and they are primarily "he's" from this era—was young and, frankly, didn't have much else going on. Working backstage sounded cool enough, so he agreed to drive the van and push some boxes of gear, maybe learn to focus some lights. Then the band just blew-up overnight, jumping from gymnasium shows to theaters to arenas, so, the production grew too. There was work to be done, and he was there to do it. All the "he's" became lighting designers and video innovators and production managers, because there was a need and they were there fix it. These roadies started specializing, and developed touring rock and roll as we know it today.

I've always heard that touring started from a family garage in Pennsylvania. Two brothers made some speakers for a college to use for concerts. Back in 1966, even nationally-known musicians familiar from the radio would play much smaller venues, like school auditoriums or community centers. They would use whatever gear was available in that building. Shows were simple then, usually a basic wooden riser as the stage, a few microphones, a pair of speakers, and if the band was lucky, a spotlight.

Rumor has it, Frankie Valli came through town to play at the college, and had one of his best shows. Energy was high, the fans engaged, and the sound fantastic. Clear, intentional audio allowed the audience to participate like they hadn't before. The next several shows, played through basic equipment, seemed disappointing in comparison. Crowds were dull. Energy was down. The band agreed they needed the brothers' speakers for every performance.

No one had done that before. No one had packaged large, delicate, expensive equipment to be moved around from city to city. No one had put much attention into the technical aspects of a performance at all, just "making do." But, if speakers could be specialized, perfected, and transported to improve the quality of the show, other elements could be, too.

While rigging his own stunts, a circus performer discovered he could combine the strength of the building grid and the ingenuity of a standard one-ton chain to support full show designs. He had always experimented with his own equipment, and understood the same principles could apply to bigger theatrics. He turned the motor upside down and snaked the linked chain over the grid. As the chain was drawn back into the motor, it could raise and lower thousands of pounds of gear. It meant speakers and lights and other large gear could be assembled on the ground and then lifted into the air, hanging directly above the stage. Now, a rigging department is on every full tour.

Shows added dancers and wardrobe changes, so people joined the tour to coordinate costumes and choreograph their onstage routines. Computers brought video content and lasers. Some roadies harnessed fire to be used safely as flair, and "special effect" techs were added to the crew list.

The bands themselves became iconic, and so did their lifestyle backstage. Fans started looking for that next big moment—the next Wall or Woodstock. Standing in the audience, waving a lighter, maybe they'd catch an epic guitar smash. Maybe a Courtney Cox moment, lifted out of obscurity to dance with Bruce Springsteen. People want the chance to be part of something great.

Concerts today strive to bring that experience to everyperformance. Elaborate designs, cutting-edge technology, and dozens of separate departments all feed into the production: more a spectacle than a concert. It's not just about the music anymore. It's about the show. Bigger and bolder means backstage continues to get busier. It is a well-hidden world that exists to support the artists, to feed the fans, and to help create the legend of rock and roll.

RIGGER

It's Ben's birthday next week. He will be twenty-seven. The day will be spent the same way he's spent it the last several years: loading in a show. This production team is fun, though. They'll do something to celebrate. He walked in this morning with one of the assistants. She spent the walk from the busses into the building asking him, hypothetically, about favorite cake flavors. Still, the day will be about the show. Ben knows that.

He pulls off his sweatshirt to leave with his backpack in the production office, until his own road case comes in later. A new tattoo reaches out from the top of his tank. Swirls of black and red map out Mars, the sign of Aries. He has collected quite a few tattoos from around the world. Ben likes this new one, but his favorite is still a custom Mauri symbol he got in a garage in New Zealand. It stretches across his calf, flexing as he climbs, and Ben does a lot of climbing.

No breakfast until after points are hung, so that load in can keep moving. All he needs for now is his harness, his helmet, and the rigging stuff off the truck. Ben carries his gear slung over a shoulder by the d-ring, as he walks across the empty arena floor. Not many people are here yet, and that's how Ben likes it.

"When I have a lot to sort through, you know, something I'm working out for myself, I always feel better if I'm climbing," says Ben. "Of course, I'd prefer to be climbing somewhere better like Zion or Yosemite, but climbing for work can be okay, too. I mean I've been doing it for years by now. It just helps me think."

At the base of the long ladder, he flips his gear to the floor. Most buildings offer an elevator to the top row of audience seating, but reaching the rafters still involved scaling a few stories by stair or ladder. Today's climb to the ceiling is longer than most, but he doesn't mind.

First, Ben buckles the strap of his helmet. Sometimes a GoPro camera is fastened tightly to the top, but he doesn't bring it as often anymore. Ben's been to this building before, and the view from the top will be nothing special, so he leaves it off. Next he steps into his harness, cinched at each thigh, and around the waist. He takes a few small jumps to let everything settle into place. Most days don't really start for Ben until he steps into his climbing gear. This kit weights a full three pounds more than any he'd bring on a real outdoor adventure, a literal reminder of his responsibility as a rigger. He reaches for the highest rung he can, and starts the climb.

Understand, rock shows are heavy. As a concert is built, the audio, lights, video, automation, and whatever the set design team has dreamed up, will hang from steel supports in the building. A lot of attention goes into not ripping a hole in the ceiling. The riggers map out how everything will fit, then climb up to the beams to hang it. Nothing goes into the air until the riggers approve it.

Rigging for sailing and stunts is not new. Rigging for concert touring, however, is only a few decades old. As shows grew increasingly elaborate, they also got heavier. Rigging became essential, and experts evolved to bring safe and efficient ways to support production elements from the air. Innovative solutions had to be invented to accommodate.

Every building has different structural elements. Each show has different structural needs. Together with the local rigger (who know the building,) the touring riggers (who know the show) are part of planning the daily layout. The goal is to find a way to hang all the elements safely, without affecting the way the big picture looks to an audience. There is a lot of math, a lot of triangles, and also, a lot of liability. Without the right attention to detail, a heavy show runs the risk of over-extending the weight capacity of a venue.

The worst case scenario: tons of gear crashing to the ground, or onto the heads of the audience below. Ben has never seen anything like it first-hand, but his dad taught him to respect the significance of their role. The responsibility of his job on the tour.

Ben's breath is heavy, but steady. A familiar burn starts in his thighs, and run up into his back. He looks down, then back toward the top of the ladder. He's only about half way. He pauses for few breaths, then starts again. He pushes air between his lips, and tries to clear his head. While trainings are important, no amount of certification will help with the hands-on, common-sense skills needed for challenging production days. Success here is measured in quick, creative solutions, specialized understanding, and a thick skin.

This is how Ben was raised. It's what he's always known. "My dad basically created concert rigging. Him and the guys of his generation. They figured it all out. They got things off the ground, and made it up as they went. He wasn't really home much for birthdays, or things like that, because he was out here building shows. You just realize that specific days don't matter as much as people think. When the tour was happening, that's where he needed to be. I didn't always understand that, of course. He's my dad. But, I get that more now that I'm doing it too."

Honestly, Ben never really considered doing anything else, at least at first. He got his IATSE union card on his eighteenth birthday, and was put on his first call the next day. His first tour wasn't long after. He was going to be a rigger, just like his dad. He knows not everyone gets travel like this, or see so many amazing performances, or meet such weird and different people. But, then again, not everyone has to sleep on a bus with a dozen others, or hang the same production every day, or spend every night after work driving to a new city. Good and bad, it's the family business.

Reaching the catwalk, Ben pauses and leans against the side rail. Over the edge it is a straight drop to the arena floor, already starting to buzz with activity. The air changes up here. Down below, it isn't quite fresh, but breathing goes unnoticed. Toward the top of the arena, the air is thicker, heavier, hotter. Ben shakes out his legs, rolls his shoulders, and adjusts his harness. The floor here is solid. It almost feels like a hallway, without walls. The railing reaches his waist, a safety barrier between where he is standing and the gridiron office where he'll spend the morning. The grid is just steel beams stretching over open air.

Ben is at home in the grid, maybe eighty feet off the ground. Once he clips into the safety line and steps out over that railing, he will not stop for several hours. This is the job, and Ben is good at it. He has always appreciated the freedom and flexibility of his gig on tour. He has time to breathe, but also time to hustle. Load-in is his own personal race with the clock. How long did it take today? Think we can do it faster tomorrow?

But still, he can't help but wonder what else he might have done.

Ben is smart and tenacious in his interests, even if school wasn't his thing. He pays attention. Detailed facts and a deep understanding of theories weave into everyday conversation. From classical art to conspiracy theories, Star Wars trivia to the American political system, he is an Internet-taught expert on a little bit of everything. He is logical, and quick to make connections. He reads off beat fiction, and isn't afraid to laugh out loud. Lately, though, it has been all about the next show. The next tour.

Below, the first rolling black cases are being pushed in. It is already busy. Stagehands and touring crew are starting to load-in the show. From up in the ceiling, everyone seems only as tall as the bottom of a lighter. The gear will come off the trucks in the same order it does at every show. Straddling the large, steel beams, bridling the motors, Ben will spend the morning pulling chain from the ground up into the rafters to hold up the production. It doesn't matter the building, it doesn't matter the city. It doesn't even really matter the show. Ben will climb. He will get his hands dirty. He will be sweaty before lunch is served. He will hang all of the motors that hold up the show as quickly and efficiently as he's been raised to do.

Lately, it's the monotony that has been getting to Ben. He spends most of his time imagining what he might be doing if he were home. He'd actually wake up in the house he bought eight years ago. Maybe he'd get to sleep in, for once, or maybe he'd finally finish tiling the hallway. He'd hang out with his dogs and his bird and his snake, which really belong more to his mom by now, because of how often he's away. If Ben were home in Las Vegas, he'd probably be headed out to Red Rocks National Park, or even over to Joshua Tree. He'd be climbing just to climb. He could get back into mountain biking, or have dinner with his sister. He'd learn to keep a garden, despite the desert heat. He'd raise bees. Maybe chickens. He might finally have room for a girlfriend. Might have time for himself.

The day continues below him, because of him, following the same choreography as usual. Ben sits above the action, thinking about where else he might be. Thinking, maybe, he's been touring too long already.

STARTING OUT

The backstage layout is different at every venue. Amphitheaters are smaller than basketball arenas, partially outdoor, and usually have a finished hallway behind the stage with offices, dressing rooms, and food. Stadiums are outside, and huge. Large portions of the day are lost walking from one place to another, and a load-in might even take multiple days.

Arenas, where I've worked most of my career, are indoor ovals, surrounded by seats. The end closest to the dock is known as backstage. Offices and dressing rooms are in the hallways off of that and underneath the seats. The public stays on the other side of the building.

Walking in each morning, production's first task is to assign the rooms. Catering is obvious: hopefully set up before the touring crew gets there, and connected to a kitchen. Usually the production office is assigned next. This one is also pretty obvious: a large, centralized room close to the action and easy to find. Dressing rooms, other private offices for accountants and managers, lounge space, and other rooms get prioritized, depending on how much space is available. As I walk, following the production manager, I scribble assignments onto Post-its and stick them to door frames. I'll be back around later to post specially designed tour signs, laminated and sturdy enough to last from show to show.

After we've toured backstage, the production crew circles back to our office for the day. Six-foot plastic tables are folded and leaning between the lockers and a row of benches. On non-show days, this must be the visiting team's locker room, for whatever sport plays here. Sometimes the smell makes it impossible to forget our desks are surrounded by old socks and jockstraps, but it's usually the biggest room, and we need the space. A bright tablecloth and some scented candles help make the space seem less repellant. Our full office set-up will be delivered once the trucks are unloaded. To get started, the bare bones of my daily desk are packed in the purse slung over my shoulder. Rooming lists, schedules, notebooks, Post-its and Sharpies—this bag is my lifeline. It once weighed in at twenty-four pounds.

The list of essentials I carry has evolved with the job.

My first day with a tour, I drove in from home to meet the crew at rehearsals. I had met the team a few days earlier while the band was performing two songs for a television show where I worked.

I thought I was walking into an interview.

Less than two months out of college, I still envisioned job interviews like we'd practiced in school. Nice clothes to make a good impression. The exchange of a paper résumé. A series of well-reasoned questions to determine how I'd think on my feet. In all, an hour or two of talking and "tests," and they would call me later to let me know. That's how it worked for my parents. That's how it worked for my friends.

I was supposed to meet the production manager, known as Boston, at ten that morning, so had set my alarm for seven to prepare. I had probably hit the snooze button two, maybe three times, but made sure to be out of bed by eight. My résumé was printed, proofread and tweaked, then printed again and placed in my purse. I decided to bring a laptop and passport, just to seem prepared. I was nervous, and didn't know what I might need.

With a second cup of coffee, I sat on the floor of my room in my modest first apartment. The main room had hardwood, but each of the two bedrooms had carpet. Not the fluffy, comfortable kind you'd dig your toes into, but a tight, knotted kind that doesn't stain. The doors of my closet were mirrored from floor to ceiling. Sitting cross-legged, I got ready for the day.

I had cleaned my face thoroughly the night before, and already moisturized earlier that morning. I took breaks to sip my home-brewed coffee and check my reflection. I put in my contacts and brushed my teeth.

That morning, I decided to wear a simple cotton dress. It was one of my favorites, green with small white flowers and three buttons at the bottom of the collared V-neck. It came to rest just above my knees, and paired with durable leather moccasins was just fine for a production interview, I imagined. I already knew closed-toe shoes were a must.

Parking on the street had been fairly easy, but it took nearly ten minutes to find my way into the rehearsal venue. The front door was locked and a fence ran around most of the building. I tried calling the production manager with the one contact number I had, but no answer. Locked out. From down the block, I noticed three guys leaving a back lot and ran to them. I mentioned Boston's name, and they let me inside the restricted area. Once through the fence, all the doors were open.

A small group gathered outside in the shade, smoking cigarettes, or something. Men were scattered around the door near the loading dock and throughout the long, backstage hallway. Each seemed to be working on his own project. One was using a soldering iron, though I wasn't sure what to call it yet. Another tightened the wheels of a large black cube on wheels, a road case—another name I would soon learn. A few guys looked up as I wandered in, but most just kept working.

I thought that arriving fifteen minutes early would be enough. But wandering through man-made aisles of gear, already lost and searching for anyone I recognized, I was going to be late. Not a great way to start.

He had asked, "Do you want to tour with the best in the world?"

I didn't really know what touring meant, but after some serious Internet research, it was like I was winning the lottery: a job in entertainment that allowed me to travel. It seemed like a dream come true, if I could find the interview. I felt a stress knot forming in my stomach. Too much coffee.

It was ten after ten before I found the right door, to the left of the stage. The hand-labeled sign on the door had been torn from the pages of a notebook: "Production." The room was a mid-sized space, lined with makeup counters, large mirrors, and vanity lights. As a theater kid, I recognized it as a shared dressing room. A chair sat off center, toward the middle of the room. Along one wall was a tattered, black love seat, where a tall man slumped into the cushions, working on his laptop.

"Hi, I'm looking for the production manager," I probably said. I'm certain he took his time responding, looking me over, trying to decide if I was worth an answer.

"He's around here somewhere. I haven't seen him in a while." His name was Rob, and he was a lighting guy, for now. It didn't take long to understand he was also sort of working as stage manager here, though didn't own the title yet. That was coming. He hadn't shaved in a few days, and his hair was somewhere between long and short. He wore a black T-shirt with some logo on the chest, dirty jeans, and black Converse sneakers. He had a charming look. While he was sarcastic from the start, his eyes seemed nice and his tone friendly.

The door flew open and Boston entered in a frenzy. A portly man, he stomped around, following his belly. He rushed into the room and flopped firmly down on the folding chair. It groaned and creaked, legs uneven. "Oh good. I forgot you were coming today."

He wasn't looking at me, but he didn't seem to be talking to Rob either.

"Well, why are you just standing there? Sit down and set up." Boston turned his back to me, opening his computer. Papers were scattered across the countertop, so I set my purse on the floor and began sorting them into piles until I had cleared a space to work. On my way in I had passed a cart stacked high with extra chairs. Neither Boston nor Rob seemed to be paying me much attention, so I went to get a seat before saying anything more.

"So, Boston. Mr. Boston? I'm excited to be here. I look forward to learning more about the job," I finally said, or something similarly polite and upbeat. Overly formal. It took a few moments, but finally he spun around in his chair, sweeping his briefcase into his lap as he turned.

"Yeah, it's great," he grunted, careful not to direct too much attention my way. Instead, he was fishing around the pockets of his bag, pulling out slips of paper of various sizes and dumping them on the counter. He gathered them into two fistfuls and held them toward me. "Here," he said, "sort this stuff. It should add up to twelve hundred dollars, so let me know what I'm missing."

With that he stood and stomped out of the room. I wouldn't see him again for almost an hour. I emptied the "receipts" onto my cleared corner of the countertop. Each piece of scrap paper had different numbers and locations scribbled on it: "July 14, $30, taxi, Indianapolis" and "June 2-something", "$60 crew food no date", "$45 no description." I looked toward the door. Boston was gone. Maybe it was some kind of interview test?

Rob laughed, nodding toward the door. "He does that."

I started by picking through the pile, trying to sort by date. Rob kept talking. "You know, if you're going to be riding with us, you've got to be the right fit. I need to learn a little more. Tell me about yourself."

"Me?" It sounded dumb as soon as I said it. Of course he was talking to me; I was the only one there. Most of the receipts didn't have dates, or much clear information. I was stuck and distracted. "Well, it'd be great to get this opportunity. I just graduated and it's been my plan to work somewhere in entertainment."

"You're young. I could tell you were new." He stopped typing and set his computer to the side. He watched me long enough that I felt his eyes. "I give it three weeks."

I hadn't been paying him much attention. I had decided to start a spreadsheet, typing in all the numbers I could, flagging question spots for Mr. Boston. Boston? There were a lot of questions, which I would eventually learn to simply fill in myself. Rob had piqued my interest, though. "You give what three weeks?"

"You. This." he moved his hand in a large circular motion in my direction. "Listen, I'll be straight with you. This world isn't for everyone. And, well, not everyone is right for this world."

He was studying me. I stared back at him, partly offended, partly curious. I wanted to ask what he was looking at, what he was looking for. He must have noticed my glare. He threw his hands up, "Hey, I can't say if you'll make it or not. I don't know you. I'm just saying, in three weeks, we'll know. If you can keep up with us that long, usually means you'll last with us a while. If you're going to crash and burn, well, that could happen too. Either way, you definitely won't be wearing a dress and makeup anymore."

I didn't know what to say. The nerves turned to fire in my belly. No, Rob, you don't know me. You don't know that I'm stubborn, and competitive, and a total people-pleaser. I don't stop when things get tough, even if I probably should. I couldn't understand that he wasn't judging me. He was warning me.

Touring is hard. And he was right. I did want to quit within that first month. In the first year, I would go without sleep, at times without food, and without family. I would be yelled at, put in danger, hit on, and tested. I'd be one of the guys. I'd be seen as a trophy. I'd be seen as a rival. I'd fight and I'd cry, and I would want to give up a lot of the time. I'd plan to quit. I'd stay on. I'd be told to leave. I'd be asked to stay. I'd change. But, I'd last, at least for a little while.

CHAPTER FOUR

11 HOURS UNTIL SHOW TIME

INKED

"I was out with that exact cirque crew for four years. I spent more time with them than my real-life friends, or my family. We shared a bus. We went on day-off adventures. We have spent hours and hours and hours together. My grandfather passed away during that time. We had been close, and my team knew that. I met my future wife. They heard about it. I smoked weed for the first time. I got my first tattoo. My second. Last month, most of us saw each other at a wedding. It had been a while, but you just don't lose a bond like that. Four years of working together, partying together, living together. We all got these matching tattoos. I know it looks stupid. A cupcake with wings. I could try to tell you the story behind it, but no one ever gets it. We get it. I know it looks stupid, but it will always be my favorite one."

Automation technician, thirty-one years old

PACKING

Unless your name is on the ticket stub, everyone is responsible for their own shit.

The goal is to travel as light and efficiently as possible, while still being thorough and prepared. There are things you will need sometimes, always and never. Being able to organize that on both a professional and a personal level is the secret and the challenge to living and working on the road.

Gear gets packed up each night in a certain order. It fits into designated road cases and onto specific trucks. In the morning, the same road cases come off the same trucks in the reverse order, and the show is rebuilt. The packing and unpacking has a pace. Every cubic inch of truck space is important. Sometimes productions travel with five trucks, or fifteen, or even thirty. In 2009, U2's 360° Tour used seventy-five trucks to move the whole concert from city to city. Taylor Swift topped that in 2016. BTS beat it again in 2019. Shows keep getting bigger and more complicated, which take more effort to move. Adding more trucks can mean more elements and more spectacle; but also more drivers and gas, and so, more money.

Strategic planning goes into every inch of how the truck beds are packed. Equipment must be available in the right sequence, so each department can work on its own elements, in its own time. From the moment the trucks roll up until the time the spotlight hits the stage, the countdown is on. There is no overtime. As they say, the show will always go on. Everything must get done.

There is a priority list. Wardrobe cases, for example—leather pants hung neatly, mascaras and shoes and hairspray tucked into drawers, mirrors fastened into place—aren't needed until later in the day when the artist arrives onsite. The tall, protective cases pack up quickly at night. Dressing room stuff is usually some of the first show equipment loaded onto the trucks after a performance, and will be some of the last unloaded in the morning. Everything has a spot, and what's not being used should get out of the way.

Cases for the production office are always in the first wave of gear brought into the building and the last to go back to the trucks. The central hub of backstage, the production team keeps working and printing and stapling and needing BAND-AIDs until the last crew member has showered and climbed onto the bus. From the start of the day until the very end, every department comes through production for information: What's today's schedule? Set list? Can I borrow your computer to print the new health insurance cards my wife sent? Can I send out for four 1-5/8 coarse thread exterior screws? The work station in production has all the supplies to keep the team moving.

A well-thought-out production case is a thing of beauty, like a carpenter's tool box. Divided into drawers, each one is likely labeled with what's inside. Standard office items near the top, as they're used most often. The second or third drawer might hold first-aid kits, earplugs, and other "there's no way you'd have it, but I could use…"-stuff. Heavy reams of paper, laminators, backstage passes, and the occasional bottle of wine are stored toward the bottom. Most have a built-in shelf for a printer. The strong, black production case, set up on wheels, held shut with butterfly latches the size of playing cards, is an office-to-go. And that's just one team.

Each department is responsible for loading and unloading their own gear. Sometimes weeks of prep and rehearsals go into condensing, labeling, and organizing cables, road cases and the flow of how the production is assembled. Successful touring vendors have perfected the packaging for ease and safety from city to city.

It's important to give as much thought to your own luggage as you do to your gear, of course. Tours are broken into legs, which are stretches of shows in a row when crew and artist live on the road. Legs can run anywhere from a few weeks to a few months. You carry what you bring, and what you bring is all you have. I did know a girl who hardly brought anything with her and just bought new clothes along the way, but I'm not much of a shopper.

I stick to a system. On legs that run one month or longer, it's one large, checked-sized bag, no more. I bring about two and a half weeks' worth of tops, a pair of shorts, two pairs of jeans and two other pants options. I pack one dress and a curling iron, just in case. I also bring a laundry bag, a corkscrew, two pairs of work shoes (including sneakers,) sandals for days off, warm socks or slippers for the bus, a stuffed lion that reminds me of home, nail polish (not that I'll use it much,) three spare pairs of contacts, a deep-detox face mask, and three personal notebooks. This big bag lives in a bay underneath the bus and only comes out when I will be staying overnight in a hotel. On legs less than one month, everything is pared down and fits into a carry-on-sized bag.

Inside the larger hotel bag, I bring a smaller duffel bag meant for the bus. With the large bag open on a clean, white hotel bed the night before a load-in, I pack what I need until the next hotel stay, usually two or three nights away. A small toiletry bag holds makeup essentials, deodorant, tweezers and a nail clipper, moisturizer with sunscreen, and face cleaning wipes that don't require water. I bring shirts, socks and underwear for however many days, though sometimes not as many pants. A scarf and light jacket. Extra socks. A headband for day three. Slippers, sweatpants, glasses and an oversized hoodie for the bus. Earbuds, eye mask, retainer, and a book I'll fall asleep reading on the drive. I bring the shoes I'm wearing. The bus is for essentials. The space is limited and vanity is not a factor.

My purse is with me always, or at least the small, wearable satchel that pairs with it. Everyone has some kind of work bag. It is filled with surprisingly necessary gear to get through my day, no matter where I am. First are the portable office elements: my computer, phone charger, work binder, laminated crew pass, pens, Sharpies, highlighters, painters' tape for hanging signs, Post-its, paper-clips, money-clip and calculator. Next, the things that are inevitably needed when traveling with a big group of people: BAND-AIDs, more BAND-AIDs, hand sanitizer, tissues, a lighter, crew list, spare passes, spare earplugs, spare tampons, two thumb drives, the bottle opener, and a deck of cards. Finally, just for myself: toothbrush, contacts case, portable leak-free coffee mug, plenty of packets of my favorite coffee sweetener, personal pair of earplugs, water bottle, gum, and passport.

There could be a call tomorrow that brings us to Japan, or a fluke traffic jam that re-routes us through a dreaded Canadian checkpoint. It could be a show day, busy every moment. It could finally be the day we all head home. Each day we pack and unpack: ready to move cities, ready to move stages, ready to be on our way. What we've packed is all we'll have.

STAGE MANAGER

"Alright, orange group, you're with video." Cody instructs the dozens of local stage hands on site to help with load-in. They've been divided into groups that will be assigned to each department to help assemble the gear. But first, everything has to get off the trucks. An arena tour like this requires anywhere from ten to thirty truckloads of gear. To Cody—whether one truck or eighty—it's all the same. He is in charge. As the stage manager, the order and flow of how each truck is packed and loaded falls to him. At least in Cody's eyes, a good truck pack makes or breaks the flow and vibe of a tour.

"Alright, alright. All orange, this way."

Walking faster than most people jog, Cody doesn't slow down to check who's following. His gait is wide, like he's been riding a horse. Load-in is already underway. The riggers are up in the grid, their motors and chains were unloaded at floor level with blue group. Lighting has their gear and their guys. Production essentials have made it to the office. Audio is almost unloaded from the truck at the next dock. There is an order to these things, and Cody knows it forward and backward.

The video truck beeps back into its slot at the big garage-style dock, its back doors already open to a bed stacked with stuff. Large LED video tiles are locked into their slots, lined up in black boxes on wheels, strapped and stacked as neatly as the crew had left them the night before, wherever that was. The video crew and the orange group line up, ready to unpack and load-in.

The crew is in a good groove lately, so load-in hasn't been too hard. The group is in that sweet spot, when a tour stops being new—the kinks are worked out and everyone knows their role in the machine—but before the end-of-tour slump hits—when everyone is tired, and homesick, and has spent too much time together. This is when touring is fun. Things are working. It doesn't matter the city, because the crew hardly sees beyond the venue. It honestly doesn't even matter who's on stage. What matters to Cody is hitting this stride as a team. What matters is getting shit done.

Cody grew up on a farm. He knows how to work. He has been busting ass and following rules his whole life. As a kid, he dreamed of the kind of reckless freedom he has on the road. Instead, he spent his childhood trapped in what he describes as a "suffocating cult of oppression."

His hair was buzzed short to the scalp like a Marine. His dad was damn proud of having served. Cody had a pair of denim pants for field work and black slacks for church, simple and similar to what everyone else wore in their small, one-stop-sign town. He used to hide magazines like *Rolling Stone*, *Mad Magazine*, and *The Victoria's Secret Catalogue* under his thin bottom-bunk mattress in the bedroom he shared with three brothers.

In the mid-1990s, when he finally turned seventeen, Cody left the farm. He had always believed he was meant for more. He wanted to travel. He wanted to be someone. He wanted to say "fuck you" to every single one of those five-hundred seventy-six residents in his hometown. Cody has only been back there once, and didn't even visit his parents. He is done with that kind of life and isn't going to waste his time again. It was too strict, too boring. For Cody, being on tour is like winning the lottery, and he has always made it a point to take full advantage.

Now, at forty-two, it seems like most of the guys he started out with have been slowing down. Some are off the road completely. A few are dead. Lately, if Cody wants a truly crazy night—outside of Vegas (where everyone parties) or some resort location (where everyone parties)—he has to do it by himself, or find some young guns to hang with. The early twenty-somethings are always up for a good time. At least the cool ones are. He'd prefer going out with a group his own age, but that means two beers then home to video chat with the kids. Cody tries to squeeze his family calls into his dinner breaks on show days. Days off are just for him.

Three years ago, Cody gave into convention and married a British waitress he'd met in Manchester while on tour with Bob Seger. Or had he been working for Bruce Springsteen? Kim was nice enough, and she adored Cody like he was the rock star with Grammys on his shelf. She had blonde hair, which he liked. Cody knew she wasn't particularly pretty. Her ears stood out from her head and her wide smile proved she'd never worn braces. Still, he agreed to pass on his number after their first drunken hook-up, in case he was ever in town again.

They met up over the years, always one night at a time, between shows. She was quirky, a little weird even, but Cody found himself looking forward to shows in Manchester. Most European legs stop there at least once, and she was always waiting. Once, she put on a spontaneous, three-act sock puppet show wearing nothing but a hotel sheet. It had plot twists and multiple characters and ended with a moral. Odd, but it made him laugh. She was a great cook, which Cody thought was probably unusual for the U.K., and her apartment was always clean. She didn't call too much between visits, and never asked what he had been up to while he was gone.

From first glance, Cody was glamorous and manly and Kim's everything. Although he was short, he walked with a confidence that made him seem much taller. Blue eyes, a crooked side-smile, and deep chestnut hair he tucked behind his ears made her heart gush. By last call, drunk men at work were always trying to take her home, but she had lost interest. Most nights after waitressing, she would head back to her studio apartment, look up where Cody's tour was, then go to bed thinking of him. So, while surprised, she was not exactly upset when she got pregnant after one of their romantic weekend affairs. As she had come to expect from Cody, he was slow to embrace the idea of starting a family, but she knew he'd come around. He just needed some space. When Kim found out it was a boy, she told Cody in a text. That weekend, he flew to England just for her. During his next long break from tour, he went home to her house and agreed they should get married.

Cody doesn't wear his wedding ring at work. No one asks about it, but if they did, he would tell them that no one on the crew wears their rings while working. That is mostly true. Heavy equipment, construction, and lots of hands-on work makes jewelry a very real safety hazard. If a wedding ring were to get caught on something, a finger could literally be torn off. Or peeled like a potato. Or a finger might be pinched tight, instead of simply crushed. Cody knows all the talking points. He knows the role of the devoted husband and the responsible family man. He plays it well. But Cody also knows that he doesn't wear the ring so he can pick up women.

It has not been an easy three years with Kim. His job kept him away nine or ten months of that first year, but Cody tried his best. At least at first. True, he missed his son's actual birth, but as Kim went into labor, Cody headed to the closest airport and was there to help take the baby home. Like many dads, he stayed home a full week before going back to work. Cody didn't deal with diapers or feedings or colic, but he did spend all of his breaks with the family that year. He'd bring little plane statues or sports figures from the airport. He planned to teach the little boy about burping, dating, and American football. Although the baby had gotten Kim's ears, Cody recognized his own clear eyes right away. He fell in love. But, Cody knew he'd always think of Kim as the "Waitress from Manchester."

By his baby boy's first birthday, Cody had already started getting creative with the terms of his marriage. It started with simple flirting, to get what he wanted. Soon cheating was only defined by sex. Then, only as sex within the U.K. Sex within Manchester. He was committed to that one. He never wanted Kim to be embarrassed, or hear whispered rumors in the back corners of her bar.

He almost left her once, for a college girl in California. He had rented her a car, and she spent spring break following him, and the tour, around the West coast. He may have finally been in love, but when Cody found out Kim was pregnant again, that stopped.

Cody and Kim are expecting another little boy next month, and Cody really is trying to be better. He really is trying not to cheat anywhere.

But he's not thinking about that now. The video truck is almost cleared. Local and touring crew fully disappear into the bed before returning with the next road cases to roll down the dock and into the arena. The empty audio truck has pulled away from the other dock. The special effects/production/wardrobe truck has pulled into its place, and the green group is starting to unload.

Only four more trucks. If Cody had even one more dock, they'd be done dumping gear by now.

Cody is standing at the center of the traffic with his hands on his hips, watching it all. He is running this operation, and it is going well. Come show time, he will be calling the cues and coordinating all the departments in the show. This is Cody's world, and he doesn't ever plan on leaving.

CHAPTER FIVE

10 HOURS UNTIL SHOW TIME

ROAD STORY

"I got my road name on my first tour: 'Sprinky.' I have it tattooed on my arm, here. See, it's a sprinkler head thingy, like if there's a fire. I had been working for this staging company, but this was prep for my first official tour. I was driving the forklift, moving all these staging decks, and boxes, and LED panels, and just all of this shit. We'd been there all fucking day, man. All day. We were almost done, all wired. I guess we were just having too much fun. I was driving and probably acting like an ass, just zipping in and out and being a hot shot. Well, I knocked a sprinkler head. Took the whole thing clear off. All this water came shooting out of the ceiling. It was an old building too, so the water was old and gross. It smelled terrible. It was my first tour, and I had been kind of eager to earn my nickname. I just didn't expect I'd get it by setting off a small fucking flood. Sprinky. Like a sprinkler. Get it? Everything was soaked in this nasty water; we had to stay hours more just to clean it up, but man, it was epic. Seriously epic. I got the tattoo later that week to celebrate."

Carpenter, twenty-eight years old

LIGHTING

The floor is busy. On the far end of the arena, carpenters and their designated locals construct the stage. Legs are being locked into decks and soon the whole unit will be ready to roll into show position. Chains stretch from floor to ceiling around the arena, standing as strong as columns, but as thin as strings. They will soon hold the full weight of the concert rig. For now, the truss—the sturdy aluminum frame to which the lights are attached—is still hovering above the floor, and the lights are being set up while at working height, near the ground. The whole thing will rise into the air within the hour.

"I was a rambunctious kid. Always ready to go, ready to take on the world. Ready to be 'super roadie,' I guess," Jason stands a few feet away from the aluminum truss. Every so often, as lighting crew chief, he needs to step back and make sure the whole crew is on track. Five other tour technicians are busy setting up the lighting rig for the show tonight.

The lights pack up and travel in their pockets attached to the truss, but connecting the entire structure, running power to each of the dozens of individual units and testing everything still takes time. He stands with his arms folded strong around a barrel chest, his feet wide. Each guy on the lighting crew, and the local stage hand assigned to him, is doing his job. The show is coming together, at least so far. Three hours for load-in, like usual. Jason is happy.

Of course, no one here would know him as Jason. Really, no one knows him by his first name, or even his last. He is "Attaboy," and has been for over twenty years.

"All the other guys at the lighting shop where I started weren't really industry focused. It was just a job to them, and I was just a pain in the ass." He shares the story as if it were about someone else. A well-rehearsed explanation he'd resigned himself to years ago. He shakes his head and moves his fists to his hips. "One day I was running like crazy, like usual. One of the old guys said something like, 'What do you want, a fucking attaboy?' Everyone thought it was hilarious. I hated it, at first, but that just made them use it more. They called me Attaboy from then on. Introduced me as Attaboy. Sent me on gigs as Attaboy. After a while, I just gave in. Now it's how everyone knows me."

He doesn't stand still for long. Attaboy starts walking the length of the black truss. At over six feet, he has a long stride. He moves quickly through the maze of gear and people, checking on the progress. The long rectangular structure is the skeleton for all the lighting elements on the show. Support rods crisscross forward and back between the outside beams. Each independent section will slide into its designated spot among the others. The unit has to be connected to the correct controls, so tonight they will each behave just as the lighting director intends. Everything should be checked. Checked again. No mistakes.

"I wanted to get a tour so bad. At the shop, I was helping prep gear, but man, I wanted to be on the road. I just kept putting in my time and putting in my time. People kept threatening to take me out, but no one did. I'd go to all the shows I could. I worked as a stagehand on my days off from the shop. I did whatever I could to get on a crew. Then, one the opportunity came. There was a spot, and if I could be in Charlotte the next day, the job was mine. It was Ozzfest—everyone has a run on Ozzfest, at some point, but what a great way to start."

A road case blocks his path, already empty and discarded. He grabs both sides, spins it, and pushes it into line with the others. "That was twenty-three years ago. I've toured with Black Sabbath, AC/DC, Van Halen, Lionel Richie, the Eagles," Attaboy pauses, both his gait and his speech. He thinks for only a brief moment. Who's missing? He decides it doesn't really matter: "I mean, I've toured a bunch."

As he reaches the corner at downstage right, he turns to walk along what will be the edge of the stage, once the stage is set in place. "People don't know what roadies even are any more. How do they think this all gets here? They don't think about it. In the eighties, being on the road crew was like being a celebrity. Now when people ask me what I do, I usually just say I'm an electrician. It's not a lie. It's just not worth the time or energy to educate them, especially since once they hear the artist's name, that's all anyone wants to ask about."

Attaboy keeps a steady pace, almost stomping in his steel-toed boots. A long red ponytail runs down his back, touching his waist. It bounces as he moves, cinched every four inches, or so, with a hair tie. He stops briefly at what will be down center stage. Tonight, this is where the spotlight will hit. Thousands of fans will fill the arena, dancing and drinking and singing. But that's later. Right now, all those seats are still empty. All those people are sitting at desks somewhere, pushing through work, sitting in classrooms, prepping for babysitters, and the concert is in pieces on the floor.

It must look like chaos. People are everywhere, working hard enough to break a sweat. It is loud. There are at least five different teams of people filling every bit of space on the floor, and in the ceiling. Each team is working on several projects at once, both setting up and troubleshooting issues as they come up. There is always something, and their job is to find it before show time.

Chain is being pulled toward the ceiling. Metal clinks seem to come from everywhere. Wrenches and hammers and cables and screws and casters and pickles and ladders and deck legs and road cases. The noises of work in various stages.

There is a rhythm. The patterns are choreographed, rehearsed, fine-tuned. There is a certain grace to it. Each piece a crucial, but separate, part of the whole.

On either side of his lighting rig, the audio crew is hanging stacks of speakers. Four guys each take one side of the chest-high speaker box and roll it under the line of speakers already hanging from the ceiling. They secure the top of one to the bottom of the other. A motor in the grid pulls its chain closer to the roof, dragging the whole PA up with it. They roll the next speaker box over, and do the same again. Lights and audio are two major show components. Even the smallest tours have at least lighting and sound.

"I originally wanted to be a sound guy. My very first job was at Alrosa Villa, in Columbus. Alrosa." A young local kid passes, pushing a case of gear. Attaboy takes a few steps to intercept him, swatting the back of the guy's shoulder with his hand. He points the case in the right direction without cutting himself off. "I was just starting out. They called me an 'intern,' though that mostly meant I showed up to work for free, and they didn't kick me out. I was so ready, I wanted to do as much as they'd let me."

He folds his arms across his chest, again. This seems to be Attaboy at rest. He is strong, and sees the world in black and white. "The lighting guy there was a fucking mess." As he shakes his head, his long ponytail sways, too. "He rented a basement apartment from one of the waitresses and everyone heard he smoked crack. A mess. One day, he stole a bunch of money out of this girl's purse and just disappeared. They didn't have anyone to do the show that night. The manager was like, 'Hey kid, want to be a lighting guy?' Honestly, I told them I'd rather do sound. They said they'd pay me to do lighting, and that was that." Attaboy laughs to himself. "I got into lighting because of crack."

Today has been a low-stress day on Attaboy's rating scale. He decides to stand and watch a moment. "When I was a kid, I had this heart thing. I couldn't play sports or join the military like everyone else. I wanted to, but I couldn't." As he speaks, his body seems to soften. He must not talk about his childhood often. "I didn't really have anything else, so I ended up getting into music. Like, so into it. I became determined to work in the music industry, however I could. For me, that was with the gear.

"It's worked out, I'd say. I have five great technicians working under me on this one, for example." Attaboy is in charge of their team of six. His crew has split in half to secure all the separate pieces of truss together. It will be time to fly all the lights soon. Circling the perimeter, they check each joint once. Twice. The same order at each show, so nothing is missed.

"It is all about the advance work. It's about being prepared," according to Attaboy. "I am super adamant about my prep. At the shop, or rehearsal, we physically break down all the gear we'll be using. We wire it, number it, color-code it. We practice setting it up. We practice tearing it down. We need to know how it all goes together. Every bit of it, down to the stickers labeling each road case. It all needs to work. It's supposed to flow. I guess I've always appreciated that efficiency. That's my gig, and has been since I was nineteen."

Attaboy shakes his head. He will be forty-four next month. It's hard to believe he's been doing this twenty… twenty-five years. That's more than half his life. He scratches his temples and starts walking again. Time to complete his rounds and get back to work. His walk is sharp. Intentional. Even his ponytail seems within his control.

"No kids. I have been married twice, though. Divorced twice." Attaboy is quiet as he turns to walk the last edge of the rig. He runs his hand along the top of several empty road cases as he walks. "You know, everyone says, 'It's hard on the road.' I mean, it is. But hey, it's hard for anyone. Even if I was home every day, it still wouldn't have worked out. The problem was not the touring. The problem has been not finding someone who cares, or understands. I can't blame my job for that. Relationships are just hard."

Attaboy stops at an open work box he uses as his mobile office. He has rearranged the drawers to customize the space he needs. The right door works as a traditional tool case. Each piece of hardware is tucked away to travel safely. On the left side, the top portion of the door is open, serving as a desk. Power strips and a small row of lights have been fastened in place along the edge with Velcro. A small stool folds up and stores in the bottom drawer. He has a list of crew, with their emails and phone numbers, tacked onto the inside wall. Attaboy has them all stored in his phone, too, obviously, but likes knowing he has a backup in his case.

A man wearing a black crew shirt and glasses comes over to ask Attaboy when some replacement gear will be delivered. Another guy with a big beard and shaved head joins them. The group decides the rig will fly in five minutes, and the bald man signals to everyone through the radio pinned to his collar. Attaboy wakes up his computer, also Velcro-ed into place on his "desk." He usually doesn't have much computer work, but has to check the tracking for Glasses.

"I'm a lifer. I will be doing this job the rest of my life. I can't imagine a reason reason to leave," Attaboy sits with his legs wide. The stool is far too small for his large frame. He rests his elbows on either side of the laptop and leans his head into his hand. "But, it's hard. I need to focus on using my mind more than my body. I can't be slinging truss for another twenty years."

He hits send and shuts the screen. He closes up the case, but doesn't lock it. It's time to keep working. Attaboy will check with his crew. With the riggers. With audio. Together, they'll send the lights up to their show position.

"I like to think I'm considered a 'go-to guy.' I've been watching videos online to get better at different internet and computer programs. I've already volunteered to cover if the production ever needs help. I guess I will just have to wait and see what happens. The key is to be ready to go when the opportunity does comes. Do a good job and move from there. It's all you can do."

KEEP IT SIMPLE

It's been said that in the theatre, "there are no small parts, only small actors." If Stanislavski was on the crew, maybe the phrase would have been, "There are no small gigs, only small details," and every one of them matters.

In live production, it's not a matter of if, but when something will go wrong. Life is unpredictable, and between the advanced technology, excessive transportation, long hours and even longer to-do lists, something is bound to slip. It's going to happen. Success is judged on how quickly and creatively a person can identify, own up to, and fix those problems. From a fly gag that involves artist and audience safety, to a call time typo on a day schedule, every big and small piece plays into the efficiency of a show day.

This takes time to learn, of course. We start out too young and too eager to even realize how much we don't know. I did, at least.

One of my seemingly smallest, and most consistent jobs backstage has been to manage the tour signs. Every day the building is new and the layout unknown. No one has time to be wandering around lost, searching for food, bathrooms, or production. The crew learns to look for tour-specific signs to direct them. The artists are trained, too. Everyone looks for our arrows. Same from city to city, the directions come in our font, with our tour logo, and usually stand out on bold-colored paper.

The first signs I ever hung were at a rodeo in Paso Robles, California. They were plain, block letters on white paper, not the laminated, Photoshopped, custom artwork of later shows. It was windy, so regular office tape was not enough. I used masking tape, stretched around all four corners. Ugly, but functional.

Some venues are nicer than others, built to be concert halls, not sports palaces designed for basketball or hockey. Still, even in a building with good directional signs installed, the tour prefers to see a familiar laminated printout. Some productions mark out long bold arrows with colorful tape on the floor, like they usually do near the stage. That involves crawling around on the floor, though, so when signs are my job, I post at eye-level.

Entering through the backstage door, there must be step-by-step paths marked to all tour-related rooms. It is easier when the rooms are all grouped together, but often, productions use rooms spread around the backstage. In long, gray halls, with no identifying features, it's easy to get turned around. Each hallway intersection needs a set of arrows, to keep us all on the right course. Each possible destination gets a sign. There is the STAGE, of course. Every entrance without public access should be marked. Every BATHROOM. CATERING is one of the first stuck to the cement walls, because people are hungry early in the morning. Other common rooms include: PRODUCTION, PROMOTER REP, ACCOUNTANT, DRESSING ROOM(S), and the route back to the BUSES.

Sticky tack is a popular choice, but I prefer painter's tape when hanging my signs. For a while I used heavy-duty gaff tape. I have a firm rule that if I cannot somehow craft it with gaffers tape, I need to ask someone for help. Strong enough to hold the weight of the signs all day, and always readily available backstage, it seemed like an obvious choice. That is, until I pulled a notebook-page-sized slab off a freshly painted wall, in front of the building representative. She handed me a roll of the delicate, blue tape, and I've used it ever since.

It took me longer than I like to admit to understand the importance of hanging these simple signs around the venue. My first leg on tour, I complained about it. I'm sure I grumbled about being overqualified about the mindless work, about how I had graduated college and all that crap. I would have talked about responsibility, and about being under-utilized. I might have even confessed to a bruised ego. But the truth was, the job sucked.

I'll be the first to admit that hanging signs is way trickier than it sounds. Each laminated label requires at least three pieces of tape, turned inside-out to form an adhesive loop. Some of the hallway corners are difficult to navigate with two-dimensional arrows. Some buildings take a significant chunk of the morning to sufficiently cover. And, unfortunately, directional signage is just one of those things everyone has a comment on.

Once, in Australia, I found myself adjusting the arrows all the way up until show time. Our offices were spread over several floors, like they are in Madison Square Garden, and that's always the worst. Plus, with long hallways we weren't using, people needed reassurance-signs every few yards to stay on track. Just when I'd feel finished, someone else would turn up lost, or confused about how some "simple signs" could go so wrong. The day ended with a $1.07/minute international rant to my mom and a solid bathroom cry, all over some plastic arrows.

But, arrows were my job. If it wasn't working, there was only one person to talk to about it. Me. There was no hiding, no avoiding. All I could do was hang more signs, and create a better strategy for next time. Learn and apply it. Learn and move on. Learn to respect every small detail.

On the busiest days, when the stakes are high, it helps to know where the heck we're going. Maybe a carpenter is bleeding, and needs to find the medic quickly. Maybe there is an insurance issue, and the performance can't start until someone finds the promoter rep. Maybe there are only fifteen free minutes to eat dinner and the cafeteria is really just an old storage room, converted and hidden out of the way. On show day, every minute and every job is critical.

Getting a spot on that tour bus brought me out of community theatre shows and college media events into the big leagues. Stakes were higher, personalities were bigger, and nothing was as familiar as I expected.

As the tour started, I was very obviously the novice. I was one of the youngest in the group with a lot to learn. The first few weeks that meant figuring out payroll (which I had never done,) organizing travel and hotels for dozens of dates (for a crew I didn't know,) and sending out for high-rated gear (I had never heard of.) There were never enough hours in the day, and nothing was ever thorough enough.

Sloppy mistakes in copying and pasting might mean someone stuck at the airport without a confirmation code. Leaving someone off an email list could lead to a missed call time. Forgetting to follow up, in my worst-day scenario, would mean crews missing meals or flights. There is a lot to coordinate, so I became a master of my lists. To this day, some of the best career advice I have received is to simply "write it down." Even if you don't think you need to, write it all down.

One of my first big projects was to create a tour book for the upcoming run. The production manager had dropped the idea casually at the end of a conversation. As he was leaving, almost over his shoulder, "Don't forget, you need to take care of the tour book. Put it together and show me something. We need to get it printed next week."

"A tour book?"

"You know, with all the information we need for the upcoming leg. The usual," and then he left.

It was the biggest project I'd been given, and sounded most in line with what I wanted to do. A little creative and a lot organizational, it seemed like a way to show my range, whatever that meant. I stopped working on the runner's grocery list, and started researching. I wasn't totally sure what a "tour book" was. Internet searches were remarkably disappointing. What could I make in two days that could impress my new boss?

A book with all the information the crew would need for the upcoming tour? Okay. I started by pulling together the show dates and the venues. I sent the list to the PM. He emailed back quickly:

This isn't enough. Where are the show times? The travel details? Where is the crew list? Where is everything else?

Crap. Okay. A book with *all* the information for the upcoming tour.

I spent every spare moment working on a list of details. Sifting through emails from management and production and travel agents, I tracked every piece of information I could think of. Show by show, I crept across seven weeks on the calendar. There were some holes, which I highlighted in coordinating colors, but overall, I was impressed by the piles of information I had found. I arranged the information, then rearranged it, and printed the pages early on our last day at rehearsals. Stapled in the corner, I left a neat packet on the production manager's desk with a sticky note saying "Let me know what you think!"

By the time I went to the bathroom and refilled my coffee, he was waiting for me by my desk. "What is this?"

"The tour book?" I asked back, concerned that it was not obvious.

"Maybe the start, but this is nowhere near finished. Come on. It's like you've never seen a tour book before."

"Well, I, um," my stomach sank to my heels. I could feel my pulse skip and my eyes growing heavy with tears. I was so sure he'd like it. "Well, I haven't."

"What?"

I covered my face with my hands. I really didn't want to cry over this, at least not here in the office in front of my boss. I was trying to be professional. I was trying to be polite. I had been trying, but I was tired and my feelings were hurt. "You know this is my first tour. Honestly, I don't know what you're talking about at all half the time! Rigging.

Crew lists. One-offs. Oil spotting. This place is crazy, and nothing is what I expect. I can't do this."

I couldn't help it. I started crying, right there in the production office. Thankfully, it was just the two of us. He leaned forward in my chair. "I forget how new you are."

There I was, standing almost in the middle of a mostly empty room, surrounded by road cases and folding chairs. I had never felt so young.

"You've really never seen a tour book?" His voice had softened, and I shook my head.

"Well, why didn't you just ask?"

If I didn't know, why didn't I ask? It was a simple question, without a simple answer. Why not ask for help? I still forget to remember this lesson. Ask for details. Learn, to be better next time. A lot of times, it is that simple. And, time after time, I've learned that the simplest details can make the biggest impact, especially on a show day.

CHAPTER SIX

9 HOURS UNTIL SHOW TIME

ROAD STORY

"I usually have a break around lunch. I like to video chat with my kids. She's four. The boy is only one, so he doesn't really talk, but he's there. I like them to know I'm always there. The phone really isn't enough, but seeing their faces is amazing. I have lunch with my kids most days, and private time with my wife on most days off.

"Oh god. I never tell anyone this story, even though it is one of my best. I mean it's awful. So awful. Like, bat shit crazy, but a great story.

"It was a day off. The kids were with Grandma. We are away from each other so often, video chat also helps keep it interesting. Spicy, even. You get the idea. Again, not ideal, but it works for us. Anyway, we were doing our thing. Like, I'm full on into it. Literally, kneeling on the bed, butt-ass naked, and this maid walks in. Doesn't knock or anything. Of course, I had my 'Do Not Disturb' up, but I guess it had fallen off when I closed the door. I am still not sure how it happened. She walks in, thinks I am presenting to her. Freaks out, obviously. I almost got kicked out of the hotel. She wanted to call the cops. Production had to come down to the front desk and sort it out for me. They were surprisingly cool. Saved my ass. Though, I did get a private memo about dead-locking my door. God. Just fucking awful."

Rigger, forty-four years old

ROAD FAMILY

The production office is busy most of the day. A production coordinator and a production assistant both have desks up front, near the door. Post-it notes and to-do lists line their work stations, along with several small trinkets, showcasing different memories or quirks. One has a bowl of candy out. Each is talking to someone, and another crew member seems to be waiting in line. This is the central hub backstage, and people are constantly in and out. Asking questions, printing, making phone calls. Traffic is steady.

"We need to find a gorilla suit."

"What about a giant banana?"

A small group walks in together. One of the lighting techs has a few items for the runner's list, which is maintained in production. Her jeans are torn, hands dirty and hair held back with a thick, cloth band. She wipes her hands on her shirt, then adds AAA batteries and a step ladder to the errand sheet. "I have a banana suit in my work box right now."

"No way, man. It has to be a gorilla. He hates gorillas." He is already looking up options on Amazon. Short, with tattoos mapping a strong upper body, his voice carries around the room.

"Oh come on, she has a banana. That will work," the third adds.

"But the movie is about a killer monkey. The whole point of surprising him in his bunk is to get him to admit he was scared too, right? We all fucking were, don't lie."

"And it's going to be hilarious." She's done, and the group turns to leave.

"It'll be hilarious no matter what, but it will only make sense with the movie if it's a gorilla."

"Shit man, you're breaking my balls here." He's passing across the back of the room on the phone. There isn't as much privacy as he needs, but what the hell. His hair is braided past his shoulders, and he's wearing the same leather vest he wears every day. His shipment was supposed to be waiting at the venue. Was supposedly delivered yesterday, even. "I checked with the building. They have no record of it showing up, seriously man. They don't even have a B. Bridge here to sign for it."

A pause to listen. He throws one hand toward the ceiling and slaps it back down on his thigh. "Shit, shit, shit dude. You said Bridges. You never said Ledger. I need this thing for tonight. Tonight, do you understand? You said Bridges… wait. No, I'm not Bridges."

Sam is texting his pregnant girlfriend from an extra chair toward the back of the room. Some days, production is just a place to hang out. He looks up and scans the office. Sam is hoping to talk to the production manager, but knows that between site checks and advance calls and artist issues, now might not be the right time. The baby isn't due for another three months, so there is still time to work out his temporary replacement. Sam is secretly hoping the birth happens early, during the upcoming break, but it will probably happen halfway through the next leg, while he is in Europe.

"I've been with this crew for years now. This production manager, he's the best around." Sam is sincere. His southern twang is thick and warm. Some crew departments are staffed by the vendor providing the gear, but other departments are freelance and staffed by the production manager. As a carpenter who specializes in the moving elements of the stage, or automation, Sam is hired by each tour independently.

"Groups that complement each other tend to stick together," he explains. "It's easier when we all get along.

Eventually we start reading each other's minds. Just because I get along with the PM doesn't mean I am guaranteed a job. But on the other hand, he knows me. He knows he can trust me. He knows I have his back. No matter what. All of us do. Why mess with a crew that works? I love that he'll hold my spot and make room for my life, because he values what I do here. This is my family too."

TOUR SUPPORT

She trots through the production office, confident in her stride. She knows everyone she meets will stop to snuggle her, feed her or, at the very least, clear out of her path. She may not be as lean as she use to be, but a few years of tour catering will do that. She has a stiff neck some mornings, from the bus, and unexpectedly lost an eye last spring, but she stays in good spirits. It helps knowing she's still the most popular member of the crew.

Tulip, the Tour Dog knows her routine and her role backstage. The French Bulldog knows pets aren't allowed on most crews. But, she's a good girl and her person is too valuable to the tour, so she gets to stay. Tulip knows it's her job to be lovable, chill and bossy, but in a cute way. She is to stay in the production office, unless specifically accompanied by someone, for security purposes, of course. She can't eat off anyone's plate, unless it's offered. She has to do her business behind the bus, not on it, or in the venue.

She has her own pillow, which travels between the bottom part of the bunk and underneath a plastic production table, next to her coordinator's road case. There is water in a portable dish, dog food, and lots of toys. She isn't sure if the toys are more for her, or the rest of the crew to play with, but it's her responsibility on tour to indulge them. Playing with a dog makes people happy. It reminds people of home. It's fun. That's why Tulip is here, after all, to help support the crew, just like the rest of production.

CHAPTER SEVEN

8 HOURS UNTIL SHOW TIME

INKED

"I got this little kangaroo in Australia. See his little boxing gloves? The Paul Stanley star on his eye? I got this on the KISS tour. Six of us did while KISS was touring with Mötley Crüe. It wasn't really planned. My one buddy and I went together. We were in this tiny little town, just north of Brisbane. You know, that whole stretch of Gold Coast. It wasn't like a normal town you'd play in. It was small, and out there. We stayed at this hotel that had a tattoo shop right across the street. Like *right across*. We had a day off, so how could we not take advantage of that, right?

"We walk in, and four other guys from the tour were there. They were on the Mötley Crüe crew—hey, that's weird—well, they were getting these kangaroos with the band's signature pentagram on the belly. Not really my thing. KISS though? Every night for years I ran the automation rig that flew Paul Stanley through the air. That was *my* gag to run. The star is a subtle nod. It's cool. This other guy was, like, super eager to go first. I always want to go last. We don't know these artists. I wanted to wait and see what everyone else's started looking like. There were two artists, a guy and a girl, who each did three of us. The girl was way better, so I waited to make sure she did mine. It looks good, but the ribs. Damn, it really hurt."

Rigger, twenty-six years old

FIRST CONCERT

The first concert I ever went to was *NSYNC's 2001 *Pop Odyssey* tour. I was barely fourteen, and it was the most exciting event in my whole life to that point. Of course, I'd never admit that. In the eighth grade, it was social suicide to seem too enthusiastic about any one thing. I'd probably say something like, "I don't care about the guys, but you can't deny their music." A straight-out lie, but it somehow justified my playing *NSYNC's *Home for Christmas* year round, and memorizing the dance to "Bye, Bye, Bye."

The previous year, the band had released a set of creepy marionette dolls in the likeness of each group member. The dolls were intended to promote the launch of the *No Strings*

Attached album, and I received all five for my birthday. To seem more interesting, I refused to have a crush on Justin, like all my friends. Instead, I'd tell people I liked Lance, who seemed overlooked, underrated, and therefore, impossibly cool. It turns out, he was just gay.

In middle school, kids liked either *NSYNC or the Backstreet Boys. Which camp you were loyal to said a lot about a person, and I just couldn't trust a girl who would choose Nick Carter's bowl cut over any one member of *NSYNC, except for maybe Chris. The fandom surprised us all. The tender harmonies and sappy ballads took our emerging puberty hostage, and stirred this weird, womanly desire buried in our innocence. They were our first boyfriends, our sounding boards, our diaries. Like all the boy bands that came before them, they tattooed their lyrics on a generation and made us straight crazy. **(?????)**

I had only been to Soldier Field once before, to watch the Chicago Bears lose a football game. Our second-tier football seats provided a view to the one we saw on T.V. and Dad seemed happy about them. Our *NSYNC concert seats were much higher. We kept climbing, as the long ramp continued to wrap upward, though we never quite reached the top. Our tickets were fairly centered, but even the large video screens, meant to highlight the boys, seemed barely larger than a postage stamp. But we were there. Over $4.7 million in tickets brought together eighty-five thousand nervous bodies, all waiting for our chance to swoon over the hottest band in the world.

Pre-show music played on repeat: "Thunderstruck," "Hooked on a Feeling," and "Build Me Up Buttercup" seemed to be crowd favorites. We went for sodas. Went back out for the bathroom. We kept asking Mom what time it was, and how much longer we would have to wait. A large, dangerous cloud rolled in off the lake and released buckets of rain to chill our hormones, but we refused to leave the stadium. Nothing else mattered. Nothing else existed.

I never questioned where the lavish spectacle of the show came from. That the band had just played Philly the night before and would be in Canada before the end of the week meant nothing. Not one of us ever considered that the storm had come in quick and angry. That men sprinted around the stage trying to protect the gears and knobs, screens and wires. That deconstructing everything, to save it from water, meant they then had to put everything back together before the show could start. Or that the boys' dressing room was up on the second floor, and they had to be escorted to the stage in golf carts. We couldn't know they needed to make two trips to accommodate everyone, and that included going the long way around to take the freight elevator.

I wish I had known then that, within a decade, I would be working with many of those same roadies. I'd be the one sliding across wet stages and shuttling pop stars and battling pre-pubescent teens. I'd meet four of the five pop stars I was drooling over. Maybe if I had known, I would have paid more attention. I would have wondered about how a production comes together, or paid attention to the gear. I would have watched for the crew. But, at fourteen, all that mattered was that when the lights came down, Justin...I mean, Lance, was waiting on that stage.

CARPENTER

"Eh, I try to stay out of it. If they want a lift installed in the stage, I install a lift in the stage. If they want it out, I take it out. That's the job. Deciding why? That's someone else's." Bryan sort of shuffles as he walks, his own tough guy swagger. His beard touches his chest, and his hair is even longer. He wears overalls that drag along the ground and keeps thinning hair hidden under an old baseball cap. Though he's not the tallest or strongest, his confidence is intimidating. If Bryan was approaching on a dark street, most people would get out of his way.

He is walking toward the front of house, or what will be the front once everything is in place, the barricade is set out, and the audience is let in. By then, Bryan will be avoiding this section of the venue at all costs, but for now, the carpenters have been using the extra space to build tonight's stage. Despite his stern, grizzly appearance, when Bryan smiles, his whole body radiates. His eyes are bright. "I've been doing this since, maybe '99. I like the big tours that last a while. Big rock shows are where I belong."

The carp crew is heading toward the far end of the venue from all directions. Bryan, eight other touring carpenters, and several local hands have already built the black and silver, adult-height stage out here, while the lighting and sound departments have been setting up what will be "backstage," because it would be a waste of time and space not to. The carpenters have been finished for almost an hour and are now scattered around, tinkering on side projects or finally eating breakfast as it switches into lunch.

Bryan clears the tunnel crossing from the dock to the main floor. Only twenty minutes ago this whole area was flooded with gear, but all the cases have been closed, cleared, and lined up out of the way, waiting for the end of the night. It is time for the stage to roll into position under the hanging gear, so the video walls and instruments can be installed.

"I'm just not a theater guy. Some are, not me." Bryan is matter-of-fact. "I did *Batman Live!* for a while. I mean, the crew was great. It was my first Jake-gig. He is such a big-time production manager. He's prepared. He's good to his crew. He always has work. I would have done anything to get that first Jake-tour. Still, I'm just not into the theater thing. Too many props, too many performers. Rock and roll moves differently." He grabs the bib of his overalls and pulls up firmly, to clear the bottom hem of his pants from under his feet. His pant legs often get caught under the clunky boots Bryan wears every day, show day or not. "Ultimately, I don't care what the show is, so long as I have a show. If I'm on a crew list, I'm happy."

Reaching the stage, Bryan raises his hand and rests it along the silver edge of the deck. Six-by-eight-foot decks are assembled into a roughly forty-by-sixty-foot stage, standing between five and six feet high. If the audience will be seated, the decks might be a little lower, but Bryan likes the shows where people stand. These decks are made from plywood or acrylic panels or completely of LED lights, depending on how much a production is able to spend. They hinge together with wood pegs, or metal pegs, or magnets—depending on budget—and stand on tall, thin legs. From this basic footprint, shows add various elements for flair, and surprise, and potential liability, to the performance. The whole thing often sits on wheels, so it can be built anywhere and moved into place. Before rolling it, Bryan likes to triple check a few pieces.

As he circles the platform, checking the intersections of the decks, Bryan runs his hand along the stage. "Did you know I worked as a maintenance man in the Redding School District for a while? I was a janitor. Like, an actual janitor in my old high school, in the classrooms and the cafeteria and shit. I never liked school, when I went. I didn't go to college. Pops was done and said I had to get a job. So there I was, nineteen years old, picking up trash and puke and stuff for my old teachers and classmates." He stops. "It sucked. Seriously. I just remember thinking, 'This is so not what I planned.'

"This big ole' biker overheard me bitching and told me about a lighting shop opening just up the road." Bryan shakes his head, almost laughing. "I remember him sitting to get these giant, full-sleeve, flame tattoos at the time. Didn't even flinch. That badass changed my life."

Bryan shoves his hands into deep overall pockets and rocks back on his heels. "I had never even gone to a concert."

He rolls up onto his toes. Back toward his heels. Up to his toes. "I grew up in the boonies, man. I would have had to drive, like, two hours to even see a show, but I never did that. I didn't know anything about concerts or production or anything, but it was a job that got me out of that damn school. I made up my first résumé, dressed all nice, and walked in ready to kiss some ass, if I had to. Instead, I found this dude, all gacked out on blow, earrings all over, bright red nose. He's just yelling and cursing at everyone. He turns to me, asks if I want to work. I said, 'Yes, sir.' He said he needed someone right away. I rolled up my sleeves and have been doing that ever since."

He's standing at a large gap between the legs of a deck, the entrance to "Underworld," or what will be. Thick velvet drapes line makeshift hallways and create rooms underneath the stage. Most grown men have to hunch at the neck or the shoulders to fit under, but it is a comfortable height while seated. Dollies or rolling stools or cushioned leather office chairs allow people to scoot around as needed. Rope lights travel fastened to the drapes, and hang quickly.

Space is reserved for the gags, like elevator lifts or other "vanishing" components. There might be a quick-change area for the artist to catch a breath. Maybe a control station for one of the moving elements, once audio, video, automation and other departments finish setting up on stage. Cables will weave in and out between the legs. Everyone is careful to tuck them out of the walkways, but one of Bryan's self-appointed afternoon jobs is to do a cable sweep before Underworld gets busy. During the day, the vibe is casual and fun, but during the show, this area is all about the performance. In the dark and fast-paced moments while the audience is waiting, no one can afford to stumble.

Only people with cues will be allowed below the decks. It's hot down there, and space is limited. The noise, surprisingly, doesn't come from above but from in front. The audience is only a few feet away, separated by a metal barricade and a concealing, black curtain. Bryan is glad his cues keep him behind the stage, instead of under it.

While he's still early, Bryan ducks his head and crosses under the stage. He stops a quarter of the way through and reaches up to a seam where the legs meet. He grabs a pair of sunglasses balancing on the ledge. Bryan is notorious for losing his glasses, so he's added search time to his daily routine.

"Lately I've been working with the Carp Crew, like this. As carpenter, you know? I like it. It suits me." He pivots and retraces his path. "I tried lighting for a while, but I think you have to have an artistic side to really get into that. They treat the show like a blank canvas, or something. I just don't have that. I don't think that way." Bryan emerges from under the stage and straightens himself. "That's what I like about what I do now. It's clear cut. I'm still creating something, working with my hands, but it's more tangible, or something. I can understand it. There are very few things I think I could truly do and be happy like I am here."

Resting both hands against the edge of the stage, they meet just above his head. He leans into it, letting his arms hold his weight. "Of course I wonder about paths not taken, you know. Wonder if something different might have be nice. A real home life. A kid." Bryan looks at his feet. "It's funny, I've put a lot of effort into not having children. Now I'm getting gray, going bald, and just wondering. I can do the math. I don't want to be the old dad, but if it ever happens, I totally will be."

He is quiet longer than he means to be.

"It's good work. I do like it. Build the stage, run the show cues, tear it down. You can depend on it." He drops his arms and shakes out his shoulders. "Or I hope so. There's no guarantee I'll have a job from one leg or one tour to the next. My biggest concern is always finding that next gig."

A call comes through the radio receiver clipped to Bryan's tool belt on the back side of his hip. They will be rolling the stage, and it's time to get in place. First he collects a few of the local stage hands nearby. He directs them to move under the stage and make sure all the swiveling wheels are pointing in the same direction. The metal wheel covers should face forward in the direction they will be moving. Other tour carpenters do the same. Clunk, clunk, clunks of the heavy, plastic wheels echo in the far end of the venue. Clunk, clunk. They all need to face the same direction so the stage will roll smoothly and no one will need to run under the stage partway through. The nine men on their touring crew will spread out around the frame, with local help mixed in as well. Together they will, slowly, walk everything to its mark. The outline of the stage has already been labeled with chalk and tape on the floor, underneath lighting and sound.

Bryan heads toward what will be the upstage, left corner. "Out here, your crew is your family. We have to be a team. Still, rock and roll is rock and roll, man. Don't fuck up. You are a lot freer to do your thing here, but if something goes wrong—" He stops, pulls his hat off, and runs his hand over his head. People are surrounding the stage. Bryan puts his hat back. He is ready to move.

"We're all cool crews, but at the first sign of weakness, we'll jump on it. We're all sharks just looking for some blood in the water. You've got to be on your game."

CHAPTER EIGHT

7 HOURS UNTIL SHOW TIME

ROAD STORY

"I swear, it happened just like this. He came storming in, angry as hell. He was always angry as hell back in those days. Like, picture him now? Double that. Triple it in stupid, fucking places that don't know how to run a stupid, fucking show. Well, he was pissed. Super pissed. He yelled at a truck driver in the morning. Yelled at the poor production girl he had working for him. Straight up screamed at the local crew head. Who knows why. He was angry as hell. That was just his way.

"He comes charging into catering. It was one of those days, everyone knew to stay out of his way. Well, everyone but these caterers. They weren't traveling with the show, but the local kind. Man, that's a crappy job. And shit, that usually means some pretty crappy food. But here he comes, stomping around, already mad. Walks up to the buffet. There are no pork chops.

"I swear, that's all it took. He starts shouting, like: 'Fuck, shit, who's the cock-sucker in charge of this fucking disgusting food?!'—stuff like that. All bright purple and veiny. He makes every caterer come out, even the guy washing dishes. They all have to stand there, in front of everyone else, just taking their punishment. Man, he could really take someone down. He gets super into it. Honestly, I think he enjoys it or something. Things build, he keeps screaming, and—BAM—he flips the buffet table.

"*Flips it*. Like he was on Jerry Springer or something. It was so intense. Like, what the fuck? *That*. That is motherfucking rock star, man. I only wish I could have been there. But I heard it all from a guy on his old crew. He actually saw it. Happened just like that, he swears. Said it was just epic. Flipped the fucking table in catering. Everyone knows that story. CLASSIC!"

Video, thirty-eight years old

VIDEO CREW

Lunch is busy. The large, makeshift cafeteria room looks nicer than it did at breakfast. Wood and plastic folding tables are still packed just a little too close, but the tables have been covered by clean, black tablecloths. Cardboard condiment caddies have been placed at the center of almost every table. Longer buffet tables line the front part of the room, also covered in black and ready to serve around eighty meals. Beyond the standard salad bar, fruit bar, juice bar, and deli platter, catering is serving Mediterranean food. The falafel is a little dry, but the spanakopita is getting rave reviews. People spread out in clusters, some share lively debates, others listen to music or video chat with home, or eat alone. Pockets of conversation pop up between the clanking of porcelain plates and the scrape of plastic utensils.

Two carpenters plan on fixing a stair and grabbing a quick smoke after lunch.

A sound guy seems to be having trouble with his debit card, desperately trying to talk to a representative.

The accountant likes to eat alone to recharge, and hums along with his earphones. Maybe Fallout Boy? It's hard to tell.

"I didn't know you were on McCartney." Most of the video crew is eating together. The video crew does most things together. They are scattered across one long table, leaving a few empty seats here and there. The rest of their team should be filling in, at some point.

"Isn't Kim on that tour?"

"Yep. Totally!" Tina washes down the food with a big sip from her Coke. She is the only woman on this video crew. It is usually she or Kim, out with the boys.

"Kim's great." Marty has been eating quietly at the head of the table. "I worked with her on the Black Eyed Peas."

"I worked with you on that show," comes a voice from the far end of the table. "That was actually my first tour."

"Everyone was on that show," Marty states a fact, piling some salad onto his fork. "The Brimmer Brothers, Hoss, Grit. Everybody." He pops the fork into his mouth.

"Grit is awesome."

"Seriously. And that dude looks like Jesus."

"So much like Jesus!" the table agrees.

Gabe sits down near Marty, leaving a seat free on the corner. He is followed by the newest member of the crew. Rookie sets his plate between the two touring veterans, and makes room for himself. He has never met Grit, but never misses a chance to jump in: "Yeah. Grit is awesome."

Gabe looks at Rookie with a side glance, not turning his head. Kid's too new.

"These crews are solid, man. They seem to really stick together, huh?"

This time, Gabe adjusts his whole body, rotating toward Rookie, trying to decide if that was an actual question. It must be, and Gabe does not hide a very bold eye roll. "That's how it works. Like, the four of us always go together. We've been on a ton of the same shows." He uses his fork to gesture at everyone around the table.

"Yep." Marty is eating more salad. He is tan and thin, and looks like he must do yoga and probably always chooses the lightest, greenest menu option. "It's better that way, you know. Even though we work for the video vendor, the production manager has a lot to do with who ends up on his crew. At least the big time PMs do. The same people just end up staying together, getting to know each other. When one tour ends, we are all available for the next at the same time. Teams form. When it works, why change it?"

"Remember when we did that Christina Aguilera tour together?" Tina seems to be talking to Gabe. He shakes his head, no. Tina is driven and spirited and will not take no for an answer. "Remember? Aguilera. The one where I smashed my finger."

"I never did that tour." Gabe's subtle energy seems stark compared to Tina.

"Really? That was a weird crew." Tina pauses, still unsatisfied with Gabe's answer. "Wait." She pauses again, taking another gulp of soda. "Wait, that must have been a carpenter gig for me! Right, I totally smashed my finger between some decks!" She shakes her head, drums her palms on the table, then takes a bite and continues.

"It was crazy! It was like seven degrees in Cleveland and they told me to 'walk it off'." Tina is talking to everyone at the table, and no one in particular. "My nail turned blue and fell off and everything! Walk it off? I actually ended up quitting that tour. It was the Spice Girls, I think. Was it?"

"My first gig was on the Spice Girls' movie," Marty says almost to himself, but doesn't look up from his plate.

"You did a movie?" Rookie saw *Spice World* in the theater. His first-ever girlfriend wanted to go, though he doesn't share that fact with the group. He tries not to remind everyone how much younger he is. It only starts the guys on a long riff of jokes about his age, inexperience, and general pre-pubescent nature.

"Our shop provides a ton of screens and video stuff for movies." Gabe turns again to the kid squeezed in next to him. He really is just a kid. Gabe softens. "They do a bunch of stuff for NASCAR, too. Conventions. It's not just rock and roll."

"I've only ever done concerts," says Rookie. Actually, he has done fourteen concerts. Nine with this crew, three shows filling in on the American Idol tour for some guy who busted an ankle, and two as a local stage hand.

"You haven't been around long enough." Marty has no idea how many shows he's done by now. At least eight a month, maybe ten months a year, since 1998. However many shows that would be, give or take.

"I started as a caterer, if you can believe it." Mo has found a seat somewhere near the middle of the table, across from Tina.

"Now that's a hard gig."

"Totally thankless, hard-ass job."

"Super shitty."

No one in this group wants to be a caterer.

"Seriously." Mo knows first-hand how tough it is. "We were the first in, last out. The day was about keeping grumpy people fed, and stocking all the buses with ice and drinks and groceries. I was busting ass like twenty hours a day." He shakes his head. It has been a while since he had a haircut, and at least a few days since his last shave. "I'd be lugging all this ice around, and I just kept seeing the video crews, totally chilling on their bus. Playing video games. Napping. They were always just hanging out. I was like, man, I want to do that."

The whole table hears this part of the conversation, and everyone laughs in agreement. They do nap and play video games most afternoons. Tina can hardly catch her breath, and slaps the table. "It's definitely like that, too! I come on this after being a carp, and it's like vacation!"

"Hey," Gabe comes to the crew's defense, "it's not our fault that we get our shit done quickly."

"Why work hard when you can work smart?" someone chimes in.

"No joke," adds Marty. "If everyone does their fucking job, there's no reason we shouldn't be able to get it done in time for a bus nap. Plus, we all run cues and stuff during the show. The work evens out."

"It's like you can read my damn mind," Michael, the crew chief, joins in from the opposite end of the long, plastic table. "We've all worked together on so many things. The crew just knows what goes into a show. It makes everything easier."

"Speaking of, I'm going to adjust the brightness level on those side screens after lunch. It looked a little off."

"See. Reads my damn mind."

"This is pretty good," someone in the middle points at his plate, mouth full. "What's falafel anyway?"

"This is not good falafel."

"The lamb is decent, and this green thing."

"It's called spinach."

"It's called spanakopita. And it's banging."

"Don't say banging."

"Yeah, it sounds like something Gabe would say."

"What?"

"Gabe."

"Gabe. Gabe. Gabe." The whole table joins in a chorus of "Gabes." This is definitely something they've done before.

Rookie is confused.

"Seriously though, tomorrow we're at an outside venue. Are we ready?" Michael uses the chance to talk to everyone at once. There is a low mumbled response. They are basically ready for the festival; they are absolutely not ready to talk about it over lunch. "Fine, fine. But I'll be checking in later," Michael relents.

"Nicest director ever!" teases Tina.

"With the dirtiest mouth," adds Marty, still eating his salad.

"Is that rigger running the handheld camera tonight?" Sometimes crew members from other departments might help out during performances, if they don't have their own show cues. There is usually video content to accompany the music, playing on large screens behind the performers. Smaller screens flank the stage to show and give fans a better view of the musicians. The video crew runs cameras during the show, live.

"Yep. That rigger is running the camera stage left tonight. He's already checked in."

"Did you hear the new U2 tour has like twelve camera guys on their crew? Apparently the whole concert set up is video."

"It is."

"I've seen it. It's awesome."

"It's huge."

"Apparently, that's the big coveted tour right now. It's a long run and cool screens. The shop said all the young guys are dying to be sent out there."

"These new guys don't understand that it's not their choice." Marty puts down his fork and moves his napkin to the plate. He's done. "That's a Jake-tour. That's big league. You can't ask to start there. You basically have to get drafted."

"That's how all these big rock shows work. You have to find your crew, your team," agrees Michael.

"Big names mean long runs, which means consistent work. That's all that matters," says Gabe. "We go where the work is."

"But that's how it goes. It all works out. Well, it works out unless you're sleeping above Angelo!" Tina is always one to lighten the mood.

"Dude, seriously. What's wrong with you?" Rookie has been waiting to bitch about this for weeks. He sleeps in the top bunk on the bus, directly above the seasoned tech. "Last night your snoring was worse than ever."

Angelo just grunts, mouth full of food. He is too old to worry about it. If he snores, he snores, but Angelo is pretty sure he doesn't snore.

Rookie doesn't sense the depth of Angelo's apathy. "I need earplugs to even sleep. Next tour leg, it's someone else's run to share his bunk."

"Nope."

"No way, kid."

"Think of it as earning your stripes."

Everyone else on the crew knew to stay as far away from Angelo as possible when picking bus beds. "This is only your first tour. You get last bunk choice for a while."

"Plus, isn't Angelo the one who got you this gig?"

"Seriously, show some respect, kid."

Angelo is still pretty sure he doesn't snore. He looks up. "Oh come on, it can't be that bad."

"Oh, it's that bad," the whole table agrees on this at the very least.

"I hate you all."

"I hate Gabe." Tina giggles at her own clever timing.

"Gabe."

"Gabe." The name can't be mentioned once without being said at least seven times.

Quietly, from somewhere in the middle, a small man with a young face framed by round glasses, is reminded of something: "Was anyone with me when I pissed off that bus driver last year? He snored so loud, and would fall asleep on the front lounge couch during the day. I don't know why, but everyone decided I should complain to production. Then, he found out. Was anyone there?" No one was. "It was so intense. He came in super mad, like, 'Where the hell is fucking Harry Potter?' No one was there? I had to hide in someone else's bunk for like twenty minutes."

"Oh my god, Harry Potter."

"That's so great."

"It's too good." The story is over. A new name is born: "You are so fucking Harry Potter from now on."

"That sounds dirty." They laugh.

"Harry Potter."

"Were you on that Ozzy run when that driver just came in and started vacuuming?" Tina is already laughing too hard to tell a good story. "We called him 'Soul Glo.' He had a perm. And his hair"—laugh—"when he got up from his chair"—bigger laugh—"it looked like that guy from *Coming to America*, 'Let your Soul Glo'." She chokes and coughs, trying to talk through her fit. It looks like she might roll out of her chair.

"Wait. I've heard this story," says Harry Potter. "You said something like, 'Do you know who I am?'"

"What? I did not!" Tina stops laughing and sits up straight. "Did you hear that from Nickles? He always thinks that's the story. I said 'What are you doing!' I swear."

"'Do you know who I am?' is way better," says Michael.

"Do you know who I am?" echoes the table.

"Are you kidding? I can't say that." She puffs up her chest and swings her arms and says the line in a deep, airy voice. "I can't even say it now with a straight face!"

Michael answers his phone. "Hey. No, no, no. Before I can say it's the power supply I want to look at it again. Yeah, I'm just finishing lunch. I'll take a look and call you back."

It's time to get back to work. Marty has cleared his plate. The paneled LED video wall has been hung behind the stage, but a few of the pieces need to be switched out and rewired. Plus, he promised to fix the brightness. "Hey Rookie, we have some climbing we need done. You ready?"

"Why am I always the one climbing?"

"You know what they say: once a favor, twice a gig."

"Oh brother."

"I'm kidding. You're just really, really great at it."

"Oh brother."

"Like, really, you're just the best."

"Fine, fine. Who do you think I am? Gabe?" Rookie gets it.

"Gabe."

"Gabe."

"Gabe."

CHAPTER NINE

6 HOURS UNTIL SHOW TIME

ROAD STORY

"I met my wife backstage in Vegas. She was working, too. I knew right away, but she took some convincing. There she was, in a totally practical production skirt, hair pulled back all messy, radio on her hip. I'm telling you, I was sold. She kept making excuses not to hang out with me: we work together, she's too busy, blah, blah. One of the last nights, she had to work late. She literally had to walk to each person's room, putting tomorrow's schedule under the hotel doors to keep everyone informed. A long, boring, totally awful job. But I found my loophole. I showed up with beer and walked with her. I've been following that production girl around for almost ten years now. How many people can say they fell in love for real in Las Vegas?"

Vendor rep, forty-one years old

NO BUSINESS LIKE IT

I did not end up in concert touring because of a love for music, as most people assume.

I mean, sure, I like music. Everyone *likes* music. I have a collection of old vinyl in my living room. I have my favorite playlists and channels and stations for different moods. I probably listen to music every day. Still, I don't *love* love music the way I know some live for it. While I can read key signatures and am decent at the piano, I don't have a very good ear. I don't write songs. I don't study chords or theory. I don't even buy tickets to concerts, anymore. Music is there when I want it. Emotional when I am, fun when I want to be. Enjoyable. Easy. But music is not my passion.

I'm here for the show.

Each live show demands practice and organization. It requires teamwork and vision. It needs both coordination and creativity. Whether on stage or behind it, above or below it, every spot is crucial and every role earned. I like that. I like being a part of that whole. I like the production of it.

I came to concerts through the theatre. I approach live events like I've been taught by every no-nonsense-director I've had since my first play in the fourth grade. I loved those larger-than-life pillars of my childhood, and feared them a little, too. It didn't matter if I was taking tickets or the lead of the show, singing in the chorus or moving props around off-stage, I wanted to be there. Above all, I wanted to impress them. We all did, us theatre kids.

It wasn't as much about what we were doing, but more about how we were doing it. Raised under strict actors-turned-teachers with high standards and even higher expectations, we never considered ourselves "amateurs." The show was real, and it had to be good. We would stay focused for hours of rehearsals, after hours of school. We'd volunteer our weekends and evenings to put in the extra work. We had to function as one if we were going to get our favorite dragon-lady to crack a smile. But when she did laugh, it was magic. It echoed around the auditorium and made us feel like stars. That moment was ours. We did that. We created that.

In a high school gymnasium or a sold-out stadium, that buzz is the same. Not everyone backstage at a concert grew up doing shows, but most would agree, the ownership is real. It's the code to the bus. It's your name in the tour book. It's cruising past security and barricade lines because of a little, plastic credential tied to your belt loop. We're allowed back there because we are needed back there. We're working, invested. We're part of the show.

BACKLINE

Unlike a lot of other people on the crew, CJ is headed home at the end of this leg. He won't fill his time with other tours. He won't find another drummer to work for. He will enjoy his family, pursue his own projects, and wait until he is needed here again. Touring isn't so bad, but CJ would definitely rather be home with his wife and three kids, and his own band. Only four weeks until he's home on break. He will have almost two months off.

He's programmed a countdown in his phone to send him daily reminders. Three weeks, five days and seventeen hours until he is back in Texas.

CJ pushes the drum kit forward until the front, right leg is framed by the gaff tape "L" he pre-marked on the riser. The kit needs to be in the same spot for every show. The short leather throne must be set to the exact angle. The drum heads need to be tightened just right. The cymbals tuned. So much of drumming is, quite literally, nuts and bolts. Nuts and bolts eventually vibrate loose, changing the sound, so they need to be maintained.

As a backline drum technician, CJ knows every nuance of what the band's drummer needs to play just right. CJ is a drummer, too, naturally, but he sets up his own kit differently. Each player has his or her own style, bad habits, and superstitions. By now, CJ knows this setup almost better than his own.

These drums should sit exactly parallel with the front edge of the drum riser. The riser should run parallel with the edge of the stage. Snare to the left, but more perpendicular than parallel. Cymbals farther away than he'd want. It's almost like a sculpture, every detail contributing to the big picture. People buy tickets to see the band and the drum set is an iconic element of that image. A good kit needs both function and flavor. Everything needs to be efficient, exact, and cool, while sounding really, really awesome. Personally, CJ likes a clean look, without a lot of excess hardware. The drumhead should be cut to the exact right size: no more, no less. He steps back to see today's setup from the front.

Bold in the center sits the bass drum. CJ straightens it just so. Done. The band's logo is airbrushed in black and red block graffiti. CJ is happy with how that turned out, too, though he doesn't like to talk about his art while he's at work.

CJ started painting as a kid. First just doodles in class. Then playing with paints. He would decorate his own drum kits, hoping to make them stand out, and it certainly did. One night, while playing a show in Houston, Frank Beard showed up in the audience. He stayed through the whole set just to ask CJ about his personalized drum heads. That night, he commissioned his first custom kit. The ZZ Top legend, along with dozens of other musicians, have been using CJ the Drum Artist ever since.

Frank Beard also gave CJ his first job on tour. They both thought it was a temporary gig, to help set up drums for a show or two. It ended up lasting eleven years. As an artist, both on the drums and with the brush, CJ doesn't like to chase gigs, like some do. He isn't going to take a job, just to take a job. He waits for opportunities with other artists he respects, if he can. He has only worked for four drummers over his whole career, and still has Frank on speed dial.

CJ circles the kit, then sits at the leather drum stool. He starts to play: Bass. Snare. Cymbal. Bass, bass, bass. Bass, snare. Bass, snare. He can't really remember if he started painting or drumming first. He's been doing both since he was too young to pay attention to that kind of stuff. Bass, bass, snare. He doesn't just paint drums, either. He likes doing portraits, and recently has been working primarily with black and white acrylic paint. He packs what he needs to keep working—charcoal in his workbox to sketch in his down time at the venue, paints for his days off. Typically, he finishes one big project per leg. Snare, snare, bass.

CJ isn't sure which passion he considers his job. He has a BA in music, but makes almost as much from selling custom drum heads each year as he does on tour. It's hard to say which is his "primary" focus.

Snare, snare, snare, snare.

This venue has a strange echo. The sound engineer will help with that, but there is only so much the team can do if the building sucks. CJ releases a long, slow breath, then attacks the kit like he is at home in his own garage. Only three weeks, five days and sixteen-and-a-half hours.

CHAPTER TEN

5 HOURS UNTIL SHOW TIME

INKED

"Monkey. Everyone knows me by this tattoo. Totally bad-ass, cigarette-smoking, pirate monkey. It's me. I use it as my tag, too. You can find this little guy spray-painted in hidden corners of venues all over the world, on a few sidewalks and old buildings. Wild, but recently this kid asked if he could get my monkey tattooed on his arm. At first I thought it was sort of weird, that's *my thing*, you know. He said it was because he looked up to me. Because I had taught him 'everything he knows.' I was shocked. That's such a huge honor. I was touched, man. The Monkey is bigger than me now, and that's cool."

Carpenter, forty-six years old

AUDIO

Mixing audio engineers, like Greg, always sit out in front of the stage, as close to dead center as possible. They get a blocked-off section in the middle of the audience to share with the lighting director, and maybe some video guys sitting at big cameras that feed live images to big screens during the performance. Anyone directly running big-picture elements of the show gets a seat inside the barricaded crew zone. These are the best seats in the house.

Greg is comfortable here at Front of House, or FOH. His console is already set up and turned on. The large, gray board is covered practically top to bottom in controls. Knobs turn, lights flash, and along the bottom, a long row of faders can slide up and down. Somewhere in the mess of switches, Greg will create the sound for tonight's show. He will adjust the audio levels of each instrument, mic and voice. He will account for the position of the speakers and acoustic environment of the room until he is able to get the concert to sound the way the audience expects it to sound.

"My first job was driving the truck and setting up the guitars for my brother's band. Kind of a backline guy, I guess we'd say these days." He is standing in front of his workstation, wearing a red Cardinals hat and a blue Pistons shirt. He is not a fan of either team, but got the swag free from venues in those cities, so wears them both regularly on tour. "I was paid to drive the truck, but really,

I was there for the studio. I'd sit in on recording sessions, fascinated. Totally obsessed. I just sat and listened and learned everything I could."

"Greg." A call comes through the radio attached to Greg's jacket which is hung over the back of his chair. Greg is a go-to guy on the crew, especially on the audio crew. He has the relaxed ease of experience, like a senior on the first day of high school or a returning champion. This is his show, and he is confident in that. The radio calls again, "Greg?"

He is casual about answering back. He unclips the receiver and raises it to his mouth, pressing the call button at the side, like he's done a dozen times a day for years. "Go for Greg."

"Are we still on for line check in thirty?" asks the voice. Most of the crew has cleared out for now, working on small projects or finishing lunch or finally taking a break on the bus. This is Greg's time in the still empty arena. Up on stage, everything looks ready for a show. The lights are hung discreetly out of eye line. Large arrays of speakers flank the stage, proud and strong. Instruments—guitar, bass, drum—are out of their cases, being tuned and cleaned by various backline technicians. Each musician has their own tech, who watches out for that artist's sound. Greg is responsible for the sound of the show as a whole. Line check is the time to for the crew to check the sound for all these independent elements before the talent arrives on stage. The techs play, Greg fine-tunes the audio balance, and they make sure everything is performance-perfect.

"I'm ready when the guys are ready," Greg answers into the radio, and sits down to wait.

"Great. I'll be right out to help," promises the voice. "Do we have our cooler yet?" Greg answers no, they have not been brought a cooler of drinks to have on hand during the show. The FOH is surrounded by audience during the show, and there is no time to fight the crowds if anyone gets thirsty. It's better to be prepared, so no one has to leave the crew zone. "I'll bring it out."

The radio is silent. Greg waits a moment to make sure the conversation is over before picking up his thought. "This is my fortieth year in the business. Let's face it, that's a long time. There are only so many of us who can do what I do at this point." He is confident. He has earned it.

"I usually work with the same bands for years and years, across different albums and tours, so I learn to really understand their sound. Steve Miller, Jefferson Airplane, Eddie Money, Huey Lewis, and just a lot of really talented people. But things have changed. There are so many acts on the road and touring all the time now. The market is actually starved for engineers to accommodate, but it takes real talent."

A man with a bushy red beard circles out from behind the stage and heads toward FOH. He must be the voice from the radio, because he is dragging a blue cooler behind him. Plastic wheels scrape loud along the concrete. Younger than Greg, he is fit without trying. Wearing his own tour uniform, he is in a black button-down Dickies shirt, black flat-billed hat, and khaki-green cargo pants, like he does most days. His step is casual, but deliberate. He is comfortable here, too.

A guitar on stage squeals to life, announcing itself through the PA system. A few rich chords in the saturated, electric rhythms unique to rock and roll sing out loudly. The notes shift into the opening of "Layla," then to the chorus of AC/DC's "TNT," and back to standard chord progressions, staccato-ed with pauses for tuning. Backline will be ready for Greg soon.

"Talent and drive. It's rare." Greg doesn't seem to notice the riff or the approaching cooler. He is not easily distracted. "Certification programs are the popular thing right now. Pay a lot of money, or have your parents pay a lot of money, to become a sound engineer. That's a great way to learn and all, but everyone graduates expecting to get that highest level, dream job right out of the gate. That takes patience and a lot of practice. It takes working your butt off."

Greg is a goal setter, and takes pride in working for what he accomplishes. Fourteen years into his career, he decided he wanted to be teaming with the top audio company in the business. He explains his pursuit in detail, describing seven years of cold calls, trial runs, and general schmoozing before getting his break. "People don't understand real ambition anymore. My dad, he was a hard guy. He always said, 'You have to work every day to make a living.' My son? He's been around this his whole life. He told me once, 'I love the job, but I hate how hard you have to work.' I don't hate it. I appreciate it. That's the difference between generations."

The cooler has reached the Front of House, and so has Hoth, though it is unclear if that is a first name or a last, or either.

Greg looks up and smiles, "Of course, I'm talking in gross generalities here. There are still passionate people that emerge now and then. Like this kid." He nods toward the almost-thirty-something. "This kid is a hard worker. He would do anything for the job, and I respect the hell out of that."

Hoth smiles back, and tucks the drinks out of the way. He has gotten used to Greg's "wise-old-man" routine. He rolls an empty office chair over to Greg. A long piece of orange gaff tape has the name "HARVEY" written in capital letters across the back. Only so many sturdy, cushioned office chairs can fit on the truck, and there can be no confusion about who each belongs to. Hoth does not have his own chair, but doesn't hesitate to slump down in Harvey's.

"It is a hard job." Hoth swivels in the chair. "Not everyone would like a job like this, if they're being honest with themselves. Not everyone is cut out for it. You really have to care about what we're creating here."

Hoth is an audio systems engineer. While Greg is responsible for the sound everyone will hear, Hoth and his four person team are in charge of the equipment that will actually produce that sound. Productions rent the audio system they bring on tour. The vendors who provide the gear also provide a trained crew to maintain it. The crew understands how each speaker works and how to position the group of speakers in each venue to give Greg the resources he needs.

"Hoth is right." Greg leans forward in his chair. It is actually his chair, with his name in the same block letters on a green piece of tape along the back. "You have to want to do this."

The drum technician takes his turn to check his kit on stage: cymbal, cymbal, cymbal; snare, snare, snare; bass, bass; boom. The drummer doesn't hold back. Without other instruments to fill it in, the deep billow rolls around an empty arena. It cannot be ignored the way a guitar might. Still, this is a regular occurrence backstage, especially for the audio crew, especially as showtime creeps closer. Everyone simply raises their voice to combat the noise.

Greg, kicking into his "drums-are-loud" voice, continues without pause, "Live sound systems and the components that come with—that includes Hoth and me—it has reached such a high level. Remember, I've been around since the early days. Technology has all come so far. There's the assumption that our gig has gotten easier. Sure, the capabilities at our disposal are significantly different, but the job itself? We still have to work to get it right. Hoth and I want to deliver the highest quality experience. The biggest depth in the highest definition audio we possibly can, to every single seat in this room. That's our charge. We have to be meticulous."

Hoth is usually quite content to let Greg do the talking, but this is important. "If anything, our job has actually gotten harder. The public, the marketplace, everyone is expecting perfection. There's no room to mess up." He raises his voice to combat the drum. "Before load-out starts, before the audience has even cleared the room, people are already on the Internet. They are already talking about the show. How it sounded. How it looked. It might seem silly, but it's actually huge. The band looks at that stuff. We get feedback nightly and have to respond to it."

"Opinions are so public now." Greg and Hoth have had this conversation before. "It affects ticket sales. It influences budgets, tour dates. Everything." The drums stop, and he practically shouts, "*everything.*"

It might be obvious, but sound at a concert is critical. Before video screens and pyrotechnics and elaborate lifts sent dancers flying through the air, concerts were all about the music. Audio engineers, who help navigate the science of sound waves, were some of the first technicians asked to accompany musicians on tour. It is the essential part of the experience. Even if every note is played just right, if the quality of sound reaching the audience is subpar, nothing else matters. The one roadie responsible for that mix is often one of the most experienced, and best paid positions on the crew.

Greg has been working in this role for decades. "It's easy to let egos get big in this line of work. The higher the stakes, the bigger the payout. But that's dangerous. No one does it alone. I tend to be a very eager partner because we literally need every person."

"If a guy like Greg can't have an ego, no one should," says Hoth, but hesitates. "I graduated from this one audio program that gets kind of a bad rep among the more experienced road guys, because some people come out expecting way too much too fast. A few months or years in a classroom makes them ready, but it doesn't."

He leans back, sliding his hips to the edge of Harvey's chair, moving his palms along the arm rests. Someone begins playing piano on stage. Hoth is quick to clarify, "I mean, I'm glad I enrolled. I didn't know what a microphone cable looked like before. I had already failed the traditional college experience. I needed something to do." He scratches his chin through his beard. "I literally thought, 'hey, I like going to concerts—how can I turn that into a job?' I knew nothing, and needed someone who could teach me the basics. I still had to learn the practical parts of putting on a show, though. There is so much you can only learn on your feet. On site. In the moment, on tour."

Greg has been waiting, literally on the edge of his seat, for the chance to comment. "The goal is to do such a good job that they have to bring you back." This is his way, offering important, well-thought tidbits in neat, practiced phrases. He has used this line before, and will again, because he believes it. "The longer you're around, the more they learn to need you. Eventually, they won't want to do anything without you. That's a good thing." Greg checks to make sure Hoth is paying attention. He is. This lesson is for him, and he has heard it often. Greg expands, "The job is helping artists articulate themselves to a live audience. These bands have been around for decades. It's their vision. I can't come in and try to change the sound. I want to absorb who they are and help translate."

There has been a jazzy version of "Moondance" coming from the piano.

"Have you seen that movie *Pulp Fiction*, where all the guys have different color names?"

"It's *Reservoir Dogs*," corrects Hoth. It had just been on in the bus last night.

"Was it?"

"Yep." Hoth has also heard this comparison from Greg before.

"Well, whatever movie it is, you know how they each have that one thing they're known for?" The bass joins in on the smooth jam. Then, the guitar. Greg is focused and matter-of-fact, and not paying attention to the stage. "I'm the cleaner. Whenever there is a big, bloody mess, the cleaner is called in. It's not what I like doing. It's not what I hope for. It means someone else messed up big, and the band is unhappy, and all that stuff. But it come in and help them get back on track. Help to clean up their sound," Greg pauses. *Moondance* is still playing in the background. "That's the thing in this industry, in any industry. Being really, really good at your job has a lot of advantages. If they can trust you in the bad times, they'll be loyal to you during all the good times too."

He takes off his hat to scratch above his ear as he continues, "You have to look at this as being in a business. Not music. Not just a passion. This is a business." This is another of Greg's regular sermons. "You have to constantly be asking, 'How do I double my salary? How can I increase my worth?' That might not sound very romantic, but this is a job. Professionals have to get paid for the work they do."

A snare drum joins the "Moondance," and Van Morrison's classic finishes in a full performance mode.

The arena goes quiet. Greg stops. He stands to look toward the stage. The guitar tech raises his hand. Greg returns the gesture and sits back down. The backline crew breaks, but stays close, hanging in the wings or at the edge of their risers. Instruments are tuned and ready. Line check should be starting soon.

"You have to think about money." Hoth has been considering his phrasing. Almost timid, he doesn't want to come across too skeptical. "If you try to do anything 'for the love of it,' as they say, people will take advantage. In this environment, it's easy to get offered free or cheap work. Maybe the client seems cool, or the work is fun. There are all these reasons they need you to work for less. You can't do that. Sure, I enjoy what I do, but if you don't stand up for yourself, especially with money, nobody else will do it for you. It's the worst part of doing something you love, actually. You have to pretend it's painful just to be treated fairly." He pauses. To clarify, he adds, "It's like buying a car. It helps to pretend you don't care."

"Time to get back to work." Greg flips a few switches on the large console in front of him, facing the stage. His mind is still on money. "The only way to double your income is to double your impact. What will it cost to lose you?" He presses a few buttons and a light flashes on the board. "Don't get me wrong, I make a good living. Still, the pay scale on these shows is off. If it's a popular band, with sold-out arena tours, there should be a lot of money to be made. As it is, things are not as fair as they need to be for the men and women who devote their lives to this." He is already shifting more of his attention to his work. He has been sliding faders from the bottom of the board, adjusting levels just slightly up and down, but stops. "It always comes down to money. What is your job's ultimate value? For us, it has to be all about earning what we're due. For the production at large, it is all about saving money. There are so many people who want a piece of the pie these days. Everyone wants a cut. It's very difficult to break through the financial ceiling that's been created."

Backline is returning to their positions, picking up instruments, maybe playing a few notes. Hoth stands and pushes Harvey's chair back to Harvey's gear. Both Greg and Hoth have their radios turned to the audio channel. When a call comes through announcing, "Backline ready," the voice squeals and echoes between the two. Both reach to cover their own receivers.

Greg picks up a microphone, which has been sitting beside his console. He turns it upside down and pushes the switch to "on." Holding the mic to his mouth, he makes a few consonant sounds: "*yeeep, yeeep, yeeep, haaaaay, haaaaay, haaaaay.*" He puts the mic down, and Hoth starts toward the stage. He does not say anything as he leaves. They both already know what needs adjusting.

MONEY TALK

Napster used to be big news, but in the age of digital downloads and an endless parade of EPs, music is everywhere. Teenagers are recording advanced level tracks in their basement, and pop culture's biggest names are giving away albums for free. Since the evolution of the Internet, the music industry has been turned inside out. Studio albums are no longer enough to sustain the average rock star's lifestyle, let alone their PR bills.

The money is in touring.

Actually, the money is in ticket sales.

Buying access to the biggest shows can cost more than a car payment, lately. From Maroon 5 to Beyoncé, tickets range from a couple hundred to nearly a thousand dollars for a seat up front. Adele has been known to draw over five grand per ticket, before scalping, for floor seats to watch her belt those break-up ballads.

It seems crazy, but the reason is simple.

Concerts cost money. A lot of money.

To start, it takes a lot of people to keep these big spectacles moving from city to city. A tour might travel with fifty, even a hundred or more people. Every technician, every carpenter, every production-mind, every accountant, every show runner, every person contributing to the final performance must be there. And it's not just the crew, but each star's entourage, too. Every assistant; every wardrobe specialist, makeup artist and hairstylist; every driver is present and waiting to be needed. There are dancers and background vocalists and, sometimes, a support band, if the main stage act doesn't play their own instruments. Even psychics and chiropractors have been known to go on tour.

Each person listed in the tour book is there at a cost. Food, travel, hotels on days off, salary, per diem, and, if a tour is really high-end, maybe a phone bill or a data plan for a few key players overseas. And that only covers the staffing.

On a full-scale, arena-style tour, the gear alone could cost hundreds of thousands of dollars. Of course, that's a sliding scale. Will the production be carrying its own, elaborate stage, or using the standard one available through the venue? Will a catering service travel with the crew, or will meals be sourced locally? Maybe the departments are smaller, or the sets less elaborate. Maybe every element is custom-designed, going as far as they can afford to wow the crowd. Expensive shows will hit the million dollar mark quickly, and could easily continue to climb from there.

Each element of the show is rented independently from specialty vendors. Audio companies provide sound equipment. Video sends their technology. Lighting, too. Before rehearsals even start, the gear has to be engineered, tested, refined, packaged, and shipped.

Moving everything costs a small fortune, and in touring, there is a lot of moving. Three or four shows per week, sometimes in three or four different states. All the people have to travel. So does the gear. The more buses and trucks, the more money. Shipping the show overseas is pricey, and heaven help the touring production who needs to pay for air freight.

Fans have grown to expect an elaborate spectacle.

The bigger the show, the more stuff goes into creating it. More stuff means more people. More people means more money. The more up-front production costs, the higher the ticket prices.

The audience is looking for a true experience. A chance to drop everything else and be swept away by the lights and video and fire, by the confetti and the stunts and the sets, and by the music, of course. What some people don't realize is they are also paying for the venue so there is a place to perform, for security to keep the crazies out, and for the blessed confidence in the production team to know that nothing will come crashing down from above.

CHAPTER ELEVEN

4 HOURS UNTIL SHOW TIME

ROAD STORY

"By the time I got on the airplane, the story had grown. See, as it turns out, I'm a highly-trained special agent, formerly of the CIA or FBI or Illuminati, depending on who you ask. I was obviously some kind of prodigy who peaked too early in life, and now, in my second act, have retired backstage. Maybe I'm undercover, even. Hiding out? Road life must satisfy some deep-seated need for movement and excitement that comes with being a ninja. In the middle of a crowded airport lobby in Spain, I was drawn to one, sly and cunning thief. Almost telekinetically, I could sense the malice in his plan. He wanted the locked production briefcase, obviously holding jewels or coveted documents. He made his move. I made mine. Sprinting, stealthy and deliberate, I charged the giant. When I was close enough, I sprang. Leaping through the air, my front foot extended, I made direct contact with his throat. Dropkick successful. The monster hit the floor. With the grace of experience, I held my knee to his neck, settled my weight on his chest, and pried the case from his bare hands. I had saved the day, the tour, the world. Or, not. Honestly, I just sort of walked up to the guy and asked for our stuff back. He put it down, and ran away. Literally, that's it. But the story grew to be bigger than me, and who am I to argue with urban legend?"

Production Assistant, twenty-five years old

BROWN M&Ms

There is a story told about brown M&Ms. An urban legend, of sorts, that both roadies and super fans have heard a hundred times. Sometimes the band changes, but the story remains the same. I first heard it while visiting the BBC Studios back in college. It was told again as I started setting up artists' dressing rooms. Again during a chat with an old lighting guy.

Before arriving at each venue, production turns in a rider of requirements that the building must have waiting. Some requests are structural, like the weight capacity of the grid or amount of power needed to run the show. There is a section about how many local crew members are needed, sections about bus parking, Internet, tables and chairs, and always, a section on artist needs, called the "dressing room rider."

A typical dressing room rider for a band might look something like:

- ( ) two cases of Fiji water 250 ml bottles <u>on ice</u> (non–carbonated)
- ( ) four Pellegrino water 250 ml bottles
- ( ) four bottles of Gatorade 10-12 oz. size (dark blue or purple)
- ( ) one case (12) Diet Coca Cola (8 oz GLASS BOTTLES preferred)
- ( ) two bottles of 16 oz POMWonderful pomegranate juice
- ( ) one bottle of Jim Beam <u>Black</u> or Crown Royal

- ( ) select two hot entrees, service for six:
    - [ ] beef or chicken shish-kebobs with roasted vegetables
    - [ ] cocktail wieners with dipping sauce
    - [ ] BBQ ribs, roast beef, roast chicken or meatballs
    - [ ] house specialty must be pre-approved

* These entrees are to be in a temperature-controlled chafing dish

- ( ) shrimp cocktail w/ sauce pre-peeled, service for six
- ( ) cheese & vegetable plate, must include brie and sharp cheddar. *Please serve with knife & cutting board
- ( ) two bowls fresh-cut fruits including at least four of following:
    - [ ] cantaloupe
    - [ ] watermelon

[ ] seedless green grapes
[ ] strawberries
[ ] raspberries
[ ] kiwi

* No oranges, grapefruit, citrus etc.—BAD FOR VOICE
( ) two sliced avocados
( ) fresh red salsa
( ) one bag of organic corn chips
( ) Spanish olives
( ) one bowl with brown M&Ms only
( ) four packs chewing gum Wrigley's Eclipse - Green

( ) bouquet fresh flowers
( ) four postcards from your city
( ) three boxes of small Kleenex tissues
( ) two pair white socks men's size 10-13
( ) two candles; vanilla or neutral scent. NO FLORAL SCENTS
( ) one bar soap
( ) three (+) magazines: *People*/*Rolling Stone*/etc.
( ) small pack of wet wipes
( ) three dozen (36) CLEAN BLACK hand towels

As I heard it, Van Halen was the first band to add "one bowl of brown M&Ms" to every rider. If the candy was missing, or any colors mixed in, they'd trash the backstage and dressing rooms from top to bottom. The story has been told and retold. Pop culture laughs at the folklore, using it as an example of rock star decadence. A silly quirk only tolerated by those who have earned their place in the Hall of Fame. After all, they wouldn't be famous if they weren't a little odd. Maybe it's a superstition. Maybe it's ego. The enigmatic, color-specific treats have been written about, but usually with a shrug and an eye roll.

Backstage, though, it is passed on as parable.

See, the brown M&M is more than picky eating and an excuse to party. It is a warning. The brown M&M is a detail. Minute and insignificant, but specific. Backstage is a construction site. Working with huge rigs, heavy machinery and high levels of power, even the smallest piece can be vitally important. If a local team or touring crew missed the brown M&Ms, what else might have been missed?

It's never been about the candy. That doesn't matter. However, other very small elements do matter, on a very large scale. There is a right way to do things, and a wrong way. Most days on tour are spent searching for those moments where, perhaps, a brown M&M has been missed.

INKED

"The stupidest thing I've done? Let some kid give me this tattoo on my arm. I know, it looks like a five-year-old did it. We were sort of drunk. We were partying in the hotel and someone brought out this tattoo gun. Who knows where it came from, but it was there, and we thought it'd be hilarious to try. Like I said, we were sort of drunk. To be fair, the kid told me he'd never given a tattoo before. I said it didn't matter. I let my other buddy scribble on my shoulder. 'Just follow the lines,' I told him, and he did.

That was twenty-five years ago. The real kicker? Turns out the tattoo kid is actually an excellent artist. He gave someone else a tattoo that night, one he just free-handed, and it looked awesome. Instead, I have the world's worst tribal band."

Audio, fifty-four years old

TRACKING THE TROUBLE

"I'm here. I'm here. Show me where the console is set up." Madison is met at the back dock door by two others from the crew. He has a backpack tight on his shoulders, and a duffel bag strapped across his chest. The runner has just brought him from the airport, and there is no time for pleasantries. He adds, "What time do doors open?"

One of the carpenters walking with him, an athletic girl with a high ponytail and cargo pants, checks her digital watch. "Only 4 hours until show. Think we can do it?"

"I'll know more when I get my hands on the system. We'll figure something out."

Madison had been with this crew on another leg a few years back. Last night he was wrapping up his final date with a new group when he got the 911 call, no more than 15 hours ago. This automation system had failed right before the encore at the last show. Thankfully, the safety elements he had programmed from the system's start were still in place. Nothing crashed or put anyone in danger. Actually, nothing much happened at all.

Nothing can still have a pretty big effect on a production, though. The automation rig froze. It disrupted the cues for the end of the show, sending everyone into improve mode. It left one artist without an end of show entrance. The big picture to finish the night was compromised. The team on site was not able to restart the automation program. The gear was not responding. They needed someone to come in and find the problem before tonight's performance.

"I'm not the one you call to go 100% by the book. Sure, I'm safe as I can be, but that's not my 'thing,' you know. I'm not who you call to always get a 'yes.' I'm not the nice guy. I'm the guy you call when no one else can make it work. I've made a career from the 'can you be on an airplane in 24 hour'-call." Madison shares.

Madison has always been able to see the potential in things that others might not. He prides himself on creative solutions. He sees in numbers and codes and pieces. "Mechanics and wires and technical things have just always made sense to me. One of my earliest memories is from when I was only three. I had been given a fire truck, and immediately took it apart to see how it worked. I already had this mechanical shark I had pulled to pieces. I put them back as one mega-mutant-shark-truck. Coolest toy ever. I've just always been able to see how things come together."

The group passes from the dock, out under the seats, and onto the main arena floor. The stage is locked in place, hugging the back wall, to allow as many unobstructed seats as possible. While empty, the platform looks large and dominating, but now it is already filled with risers, instruments and props, leaving only narrow hallways backstage and a manageable performance space. Along the front, downstage edge, barricade is being linked together to keep fans in the audience and away from the working parts of the show.

Madison is lead around the back, gear-made hallway behind the stage. As they reach the center point, they turn to follow a yellow gaff-taped arrow between two thick curtains into the work space beneath the whole production. The automation gear is located about mid-stage on the far right, glowing with stoplight colors. Cables are plugged in by rows running up the back side, with two large screens sitting at the front. The large, elevator-type machine in trouble is stationed within eye sight of the controls, supposedly, ready to raise and lower at varying speeds throughout the show.

"Everything is plugged in where it should be. We've rebooted. We've tried the shortcut codes. We've all tried all our *tricks*, you know," the girl reaches up to tighten her ponytail. "It was working through the last show, until the very end. We went into response mode in the moment. We spent more time then we should have trying to trouble shoot during load out. Nothing."

A guy, chewing gum, nods in agreement. He is young, though not as young as Madison was when he started. "I was sort of hoping it would just work today when we put it all back together. Nope."

That does happen. Sometimes just turning it off and on does work, who knows why, but not here. They wouldn't have called Madison if it was that easy. He drops his bag, and crouches in front of the tall, black case. A big guy by anyone's scale, as Madison bends to balance on his toes in thick work boots, the case seems to dwarf behind him. He will figure this out. Only thirty-five, Madison's hair and beard are already a rich silver. He rubs his head and drops one knee down to the floor. Leaning onto his opposite knee, he takes a closer look at the bottom row of inputs.

One of the adapters looks a little wobbly. He reaches into his pocket and pulls out a newer one. He laughs to himself. He has been carrying spare parts with him since he was a kid. No one could guess how many times something he just "happens to have" has saved his ass, on shows and in real life. A surprising 5-pin to 3-pin adapter swap made him crew-famous on his first big stadium tour when he caught a malfunction and fixed it just moments before showtime. The boy band and the audience never knew something was wrong, because Madison thought quickly and had what he needed. That save earned him three more big tours with that production manager, and a few life long friends who celebrated him like a hero on the bus that night.

It doesn't seem to be the adapter this time, but it was worth a shot. Madison takes his time to stand. He hurt his ankle pretty badly on tour a few years back, and has to be more mindful these days. "It's actually one of the few situations I haven't had a back-up plan for. I started in this industry so young. I love it. My lady tours too. This is my world, my life, you know? One group of guys where they shouldn't have been during load out in London, though? Just one misstep off the back of the stage? Literally, one moment and it all changed. It could have been so much worse. People have died in similar falls, but that shattered ankle put me out of work for almost two years. Multiple surgeries, physical therapy, a lot of pain. I walked with a cane, like I was eighty-five. You can't tour like that. It's the longest I had been home since I was a teenager. I really started thinking I might never get to go out again."

Madison follows the chunky, black cables out the back of the console. He checks the power transformer switch. That is another usual culprit in problem moments. The machine needs to work on various power levels around the world, and won't work if it's set in the wrong mode. Again, not the problem here. He moves to the front of the console, and settles into one the padded office chairs to start up the computer. Must be a problem with the interface there. Methodical and deliberate, Madison tries not to get too ahead of himself. The problem is right in front of him, he just needs to find it. Find it and fix it.

"I couldn't jump right back into touring without some changes. With an injury like that, I knew I wouldn't be able to do my gig exactly like I had been doing it. The job had to adjust, and so did I. Sometimes it's basic stuff, like changing my socks more and trying to exercise. I buy new shoes more often now, for better support. But it's more than that. I can't be the macho young guy who carries everything at load out. I can't crawl around like I use to. I have to trust the other people on my team more. That was the hardest adjustment. I'm not always going to be the guy out front, passing everyone up. I had to learn that was okay. I don't have to do it all. I need to do my piece. I show up. I do my job. I trust that others will too, without me doing it all. If they need me, they'll ask, you know."

A voice comes through the receiver on both crew radios, "Is Madison here yet?" It's either the crew chief, or the production manager. The touring team sends back a yes, and assures that Madison is already working on a fix. "We only have a few hours. If we are going to cut these gags, we have to start telling everyone soon. Does he think he can do something before the show?"

"Tell him I need another half an hour. This isn't really acting like an electrical problem. I'm checking the programming now. We'll see." answers Madison, then adds, "We'll have time to write a few new cues if we really need to."

Tensions are always heightened when big artist elements are on the line, especially this close to show time. The performers have a choreography they depend on, and so does the crew. One leads to the next, connected. Getting that sequence perfect is always the goal. But, the audience is already headed toward the venue, and with or without all the extras, the show will happen. The crew will find a workable solution. That's the job.

The keyboard clicks beneath Madison's fingers, nails clean and trimmed. His hands are always washed. Typing continues in rhythm. A few strokes. A few more. Pause. Click, click, click. Pause. It's hard to tell from his concentrated expression if knows what he's looking for, but Madison remains composed.

Not everyone appreciates the pressure of high stakes like a show day, but this is where Madison thrives. Adrenaline is coursing, the mind is racing through possible solutions, the clock is counting down. This moment is what he can't find in other jobs. This moment is what keeps Madison on tour; this high is what keeps most road crew coming back, he'd expect.

Madison has been chasing the rush of live shows since middle school, where he tasked himself with rewiring his first few lights for a community theatre. He moved from the lights to the lighting console. "Playing," as he describes it, he had fun experimenting with the gear to understand how it all worked together, but seeing the tangible impact at the actual show is what sealed the deal. Madison was only ten, but knew he'd found his niche. At fourteen, he convinced a family friend who drove trucks for productions to take him backstage at his first concert. By seventeen, he took his first touring job and has worked in nearly every department since. While young, Madison has already been touring over half his life.

"Of course I wonder what else I might have done, and I almost had to find out. I mean, there are other jobs out there. I graduated high school early with significant college credits toward a degree in physics, so I could explore that. But while I was stuck home, I realized very quickly how much I'd miss all this. Sure, the specifics might change. I've done so many gigs, with so many crews, on so many tours. In the end, just being out here is the job I want. I want the show day. I want the audience. I want the last minute problems. I want the crews, or, most crews. This is my world. I haven't really known anything else."

Madison spins his chair at the makeshift desk to watch the large piece of gear, still sitting fixed and quiet. Without looking, he hits a few more keys, then pauses. A few more. And, again. He turn his full attention to the screen, and begins typing quickly. Everyone stands around him, waiting to hear a diagnosis. His fingers seem to be commanding the keys to attention, as the machine finally groans to life.

"Here it comes!" The gum chewer responses quickly. Everyone turns to watch. It doesn't move much, but the response means progress for Madison.

"Well, it's alive," Madison agrees. "I'd say we don't need to order any gear. That's a good thing, and definitely makes for a faster fix. But it looks like the system was been wiped, somehow. It sucks, but everything in this system is connected. We'll have to reprogram the whole show to make sure nothing was missed."

The female carpenter checks her watch again, and makes a face. "That doesn't sound like a quick fix."

"Nope, the regular automated cues will not run tonight," confirms Madison, as he leans back in the chair.

She brings her hands to her hips and looks the large gag up and down, shaking her head, then turns back toward Mr. Fix-It. "Okay, so what can we make happen for tonight?"

Madison smiles. That's what he loves about touring crew. The show will always go on, somehow. He reaches for his bag, to get his tool belt. "We won't be able to do everything, so let's pick the most crucial show moments to focus on. I'll program some custom moves. You'll need some extra bodies here tonight for safety, but with a manual jog or two, we will make something happen. The show back up to normal for the next performance."

She nods her head, it's only a couple hours until the show. They have to work quickly. They leave the youngest a few tasks, and head toward the production office to pass their findings up the ladder so everyone knows the new plan. One change effects everyone, and communication is key.

"One way or another, things seem to turn out. I had to learn that sometimes it might not be perfect. Sure, we aim for that, but sometimes we have to get a little creative and 'pretty perfect' is good enough. Though, I know I'm lucky. If I take things one part at a time, I can usually trust the problem will work itself out," he offers humbly, yet as a matter of fact. "Well, except with mitered corners. Whatever I do, I can't seem to get those," he adds, though it's unclear if it's a joke, or a confession. "That, and never trust my spelling."

CHAPTER TWELVE

3 HOURS UNTIL SHOW TIME

ROAD STORY

"It was super early in the morning. We had stayed in some fancy hotel that night. We had done a walk away, like, we didn't have to do a load-out the night before. Of course, that meant some of us went out. It was one of those nights where 'only one' turned into a four a.m. run to Steak & Shake.

"Either way, I'm hungover. Had barely slept. In desperate need of a coffee, but forgot my little breakfast voucher thingy in my room. Get in an elevator going down instead of back up. Remember, I'm like, freaking hungover. All this riding around was brutal. I remember, my head was leaning on the cold wall because I totally thought I might heave-it all over the elevator. I didn't even move when some old dude got on at the lobby. I figured he saw my tour jacket, you know, when he looked over and said, 'Good show last night.' I nodded, and grunted something like, 'Glad you liked it.'

"It was Roger Freakin' Waters. Literally. You know, from like, the Roger Waters tour I was working on. I still cringe, ten-something years later. I didn't even connect it until that night, when he was up on the freaking stage. Funny, I would have told you I knew him. Nope. He knew me, but I didn't know him. Crazy, a little embarrassing, still one of my best stories to tell."

Audio Tech, thirty-four years old

DRESSING ROOMS

No one believes Jessica is old enough to have so much experience. She bounces around with a youthful exuberance and playful immaturity. Once, a backline guy guessed she was in her "early to mid-twenties," although she had already been touring almost that long. She always acts as young as they assume she is, and has never revealed her real birthday.

Strapping on a pair of rollerblades, Jessica doesn't realize this speaks to her real age more than anything. Younger kids sometimes use scooters or skateboards to get around big venues. Some crew guys bring bikes. Some artists use Segways or golf carts. There are forklifts and rolling road cases. The backstage hall just before show is worse than big-city-borough driving.

Some productions hate her blades, even tell her not to use them, but Jessica is confident on the inlines. She has been skating since the early nineties, and can weave in and out of traffic while carrying a tub of ice or a plate of hot food. Every second counts this time of day and she needs to be everywhere at once. The rollerblades help her get from the stage to catering to buses to the dressing rooms much faster than walking.

The wardrobe cases are some of the last unloaded from the trucks. There is a lot less prep and a lot more time before the artists will even arrive on site. Large black cases open up to reveal a full, portable wardrobe. Elaborate rock and roll outfits and costume regulars hang from a rod running along the top. Custom-made leather pants; flowing shirts with fringe; feathered headbands and hats; sometimes it's sequined dresses; sometimes they are expensive, revealing leotards; sometimes they are elaborate, hand-made costumes, on theme with the show. Tucked into the long drawer along the bottom are makeup cases, sewing kits, some home decor, spare shoes and socks, some brand-specific artist essentials, BAND-AIDs, cotton balls, and Jessica's reliable pair of Roller Derby adjustable inline skates.

Technically, the case is designated for artist use, but Jessica is the only one who ever opens it. When the musicians arrive, everything they need will already be laid out, neat and show-ready. Jessica is in charge of setting up the dressing rooms, as well as a few other odd jobs around production. She hangs some pipes and drapes to camouflage the locker room. She puts out throw pillows and lights candles and sets out all the rider items. The goal is consistency. Jessica makes sure the artists' dressing rooms have the same quality and cozy vibe, no matter where in the world they're playing.

Most of Jessica's day is spent alone, but she doesn't mind. This is Jessica's own little corner of the venue, and she likes it that way. She had graduated college with a degree in marketing. In what feels like another life, she worked in an office, wearing a suit and making copies for people. She was lonely, and bored, and felt like life was passing her by. But here on tour? This is where she found herself.

Jessica has all the freedom she could want in her show day. Mornings are slow, almost relaxed. Jessica sits and eat a real meal, and plays with her phone, and checks her horoscope, and texts all her friends, and post pictures for all of her social media followers. Once her gear arrives, she is busy in short, concentrated bursts. Jessica can be creative and organized and supportive to her team, while still being herself. She manages her own time, her own projects, and no one cares how. That's her favorite part.

Local catering or venue representatives leave the rider requests waiting in the dressing rooms after lunch. Jessica puts food in bowls and arranges the table to look pretty. She hems a pair of pants, adds a cool new patch to a vest, steams tonight's shirt. She stays in her black velour sweatpants and matching hoodie "pajamas," sometimes all day. She has a set with a white stripe to match her nose ring, and a set with a purple stripe to match her hair, at least this month.

Jessica always makes a point of checking in with the rest of the crew throughout the day. It's important there is someone on the tour watching out for everyone's well-being. Some need a Mama Bear, others need a gossip buddy, or someone to remind them to eat. True, some guys on the tour need her to play their leading lady, to offer some harmless flirtation, something to look forward to, but it brightens Jessica's day, too. Some other women on tour try not to play favorites like that, but why not?

True, people talk. Touring crews are like small towns, and the maturity level drops as the length of the day increases. It used to bother her, when she was younger. Most of what she'd hear wasn't even true, but whatever. Part of getting older is understanding she gets to live her life however she wants. She can keep piercing her ears and staying up late and getting tattoos, like the "Good Morning Beautiful" she added last month on a whim, to compliment herself, or the smiling-sunglass-wearing-sun on her thigh. Jessica knows who she likes, who she really likes, and who is just a waste of time. She can't worry about who else is assuming what. She knows what's real. The gossips are going to gossip, regardless of the truth. Jessica might as well do what she wants. She might as well have some fun.

And Jessica does have fun on the road. She's adopted the motto "always stay on tour," and makes all her decisions around that goal. What's not to love? As long as she gets her jobs done, Jessica basically gets to do whatever she wants. She gets to be social and creative, and her clothes don't get dirty.

After a late lunch, Jessica really gets to work. It's time to set up the quick-change near the stage, for a little privacy during costume changes. She needs to make sure the hot food is hot and the dressing room cold when the band arrives. She needs to be ready to put the groceries from the runner onto the artist buses during the show. She has to loop past the carpenters, and finally accept that day-off-date with Brisket. He's asked her about a dozen times by now. Jessica stands up on the thin line of wheels, sliding them forward and back to gain her balance. Time to move.

RUNNER

As a local runner, it's Brett's job to know the cheapest, fastest places to find whatever. Brett knows what the tour needs. With this many buses? That's at least thirty cases of water, twelve packs of deli meat, eight loaves of bread, two trips to the hardware store, two trips to the liquor store, probably a trip for office supplies, and at least one seemingly random visit to either a party store, craft store, or a cash/checking facility. No one on the crew has time to leave the venue to run errands, for themselves or the show, so Brett is here to do the running. He's a runner.

He likes his job. He is always working with new crews on new shows, sometimes three or four different tours a week. He sees the same faces come through a few times a year, and many remember him. He knows all the cashiers around the venue, so, in a hurry, can skip almost any line.

He's not quite a roadie, but he knows he is still part of the show. Brett takes that seriously.

He has gotten very good at his job over the last eight years he's been running errands professionally. He is resourceful. He knows the community, and can arrange or find anything, at almost any time. When a show needs, say, a heavy-duty safe at 11 p.m. on a Sunday, chances are, Brett knows a guy. These are the times when Brett likes his job the most, when he can fix the unfixable. It seems small, but he knows his expertise is an important part of the daily flow. That, he loves.

He tries not to, but Brett can't help but think about what tour life might be like, if he were to actually travel *with* the band. He's heard stories of local guys getting picked up along the way. They are too good to leave behind, maybe, or somebody quits. He's ready, if a production ever asks him to join their crew. He knows exactly what everyone needs, and how to ask for it without sounding like a jerk. He's been watching and learning, and waiting. When they ask—if they ever ask—he's ready to leave today.

CHAPTER THIRTEEN

2 HOURS UNTIL SHOW TIME

ROAD STORY

"Most intense moment on tour? We were in Australia, and the crowd was crazy. Like, so jacked. We started in on that one big song, literally the most popular song in the world that week, and an already hyped crowd just swelled. I surf. That's the best way I can describe it. They were pulsing and, I swear, growing. The energy in the arena, both on and off stage, is still my all-time high. There was this heavy feeling, like something was about to surge. Lights were flashing. These big color blocks swinging around the room. Then the crowd started pushing. That little line of aluminum barricade can only do so much, and the local security team was understaffed. The song was building and building, like it did every night. The audience was pushing and pushing. It was the weirdest thing, but a group of us basically felt it. Anticipated it. The song continued to build, and build, and then, for maximum dramatic impact, stopped abruptly. Almost on cue, this barricade gave way. Before I realized what was happening, I was standing shoulder to shoulder with a dozen other ladies and dudes from the tour. It wasn't anything we talked about, or were told to do. We were all just there. We held the line. The band kept playing. It was our little chain of crew verse this whole sea of people, and we held them off through the end of the show. Scary, beautiful, damn near spiritual. I'll remember that feeling until the day I die."

Carpenter, fifty-one years old

OUT OF THE SPOTLIGHT

It is not as loud backstage as people might imagine. Standing in front of the speakers will leave ears echoing for days, but there is a break, just behind the barricade, where the sound dies off and the noise is more manageable. Glow tape marks the floors and curtains as best it can. Colors for one show may be laid out in, say, pink, but scraps of orange, yellow, and green remain from other productions. Mostly it is used to highlight piles of cables or steps to watch for. Still, the tape doesn't help as much as it needs to. Big rods of light swoop back and forth over the stage on cue, but most of the pathways immediately behind the stage require a flashlight.

There are moments of quiet planned into a performance, to accentuate the excitement. Parts where the sound builds in intensity to support it. A live experience is meant to engulf the senses the way records and videos can't. The audience will scream, clap, and sing along. Instruments, belt notes, special effects, all adding to the noise.

And then, blackout. Quiet.

In between songs, for effect, the arena shuts to black. Cell phones flicker. Light from the venue hallways drifts in. Exit signs. Screens held up, illegally recording. Safety lights. Glow sticks. Out in front of the stage, it's more of a gray-out.

Backstage, the darkness is powerful. Heavy, velvet curtains reach from floor to ceiling, arranged to eliminate any light sneaking in from the fluorescent hallways. We wear black to blend into these shadowy corners. Our work is designed to remove any no-show distractions for the audience. With everything shrouded, when the lights drop, any distinguishable features are swallowed into the dark.

I started carrying a flashlight midway through the first leg of my first tour. We were playing a show in Singapore and we couldn't find a very special hat. The crowd was pulsing and waiting, but the crew all knew we couldn't start the next song without this hat. I was sent searching, trying to beat the cue, and running where I shouldn't have been. As the lights shut off, my foot caught on a loose cable, pulling my toes. I flung, face-first, trying to remember what had been ahead in my path. It was still black as I hit the ground, skidding against some plywood on the floor and rolling up onto my shoulder.

I couldn't see my legs, but could tell there was a tear in my jeans, and maybe a little blood. I couldn't see my palms, though I felt them rough and throbbing. I couldn't see my fingers, but there was definitely a splinter that would stay stuck deep in my hand for weeks.

The blackout will only last for a moment. The next lighting cue is programmed to turn the arena blue, red, or white. The next song will start, and individuals will reappear, bathed in light. But in that one moment, sitting on a road case or flying through the air in crisis, everything is wrapped together in the dark pause between beats.

LIGHTING DIRECTOR

No work is allowed to happen on stage, or within ear- or eyeshot, once the doors open and the audience enters the venue. The scene must be set. The allure of the spectacle might be dampened if a concert-goer saw the work behind the curtain. The crew mostly clears out. Dinner is ready. This is the last break of the day for most.

Activity out in the house has already started to pick up. Arena staff arrives in matching outfits to man the food and beer carts. A few VIP guests take advantage of their connections and are granted early access to wander, awestruck. Venue security starts moving into place, setting up credential checkpoints along the way. Only certain people are welcomed in certain places. People working out front, checking tickets or maybe serving food in a guest suite aren't allowed back behind the stage. The touring crew, of course, is free to go anywhere, except maybe the artists' prep area.

Outside, traffic is growing thicker and small clumps of the audience begin waiting eagerly, though the zealots have been here for hours. A track of energetic, crowd-rousing songs starts on a loop through the speakers. This is pre-show, pre-doors.

Some people on the road start to forget how cool this moment is. What is a dream come true to all those fans waiting in line can easily become mundane backstage. Cosmo has been backstage for almost forty years. Every show day, as the lighting director heads to his station at FOH, he tries to think of the thousands of people getting excited for the show. The fans battling rush hour to make it on time. All the money and energy everyone is spending, just to have an amazing night with their favorite band. As he walks, Cosmo reminds himself: *I am so fortunate. Look where I am. I am part of creating an iconic rock and roll show. This is awesome.*

Cosmo is dressed in one of his quintessential Hawaiian shirts, or "Aloha shirts," he explains with a proud confidence. Cosmo is known for his casual vacation look, and wears a different bold print every day. He doesn't have cues at the stage, so doesn't have to worry about blending in, and can wear whatever he wants. Today Cosmo's in blue, with large fish—maybe trout—printed at various angles, as if they are swimming on his shirt. His long, brown hair is partially hidden under a Miami Dolphins hat. This is Como's look, on or off the road: colorful and charismatic.

"I love bigger than life things. I always have." As the show's lighting director, Cosmo is responsible for running all the lights during the show. "I saw KISS in 1976 at the Lakeland Civic Center in Florida. It was my first concert, and it all seemed so huge." He talks as he walks toward the private barricaded section in front of the stage. Cosmo likes to eat dinner early and make it to his seat before the audience is allowed in. He sits in his favorite chair, with his name printed on the back, and feels the energy build as fans fill in around him. He likes the energy but he hates pushing through the thick crowd of people that presses closer and closer to the stage as start time approaches. Sitting in his spot, he smiles. "Compared to the concert we put on every night, that KISS concert was such a small, simple show. They all were, back then. I mean, things have just changed. Grown. Millions of people around the world know this show is happening tonight. I can never forget that." He sounds humbled. "These concerts are events. They bring people together. It's important to keep life in perspective. I love what I do, and I really try to remember how lucky I am."

This ritual pause is important. Every night, before the show starts, he tries to savor the moment. He remembers what it was like, just starting out. He remembers that he started as a zealot himself.

Cosmo got his first job as Falcon Eddy's drum tech for a short run in 1979. "After that, all I wanted to do was go on the road. I started working as a local stagehand. I gave my number out to anyone and everyone. I would have been happy to do anything. It was really a fascinating time for music. I was so hungry for it. For the lifestyle."

He turns on the console. He knows his crew has all the lights in place. The truss is hung just right. The show is already programmed into the buttons on his board. All that is left to do is run the cues in real time, in front of the fans. He is in charge of the big picture for the audience, and that responsibility seems tangible to Cosmo. He laughs, admitting, "Honestly, I got into lights because of sheer boredom!"

He leans back and rests his arms behind his head. "As a local, one of my jobs was a lot of pushing boxes. I hated pushing boxes. I started noticing that the first people to start working on the actual stage and stop pushing boring boxes were the lighting guys. First in, last out, with more of the work I actually liked doing? Sounded good to me. I decided to learn about lights."

A tour security guard walks out past Cosmo's booth, crossing to reach the main, public corridor. He nods his head and raises a hand. Everyone knows the man in the Aloha shirt, and he makes it a point to know as many people on the crew as he can. He doesn't usually reach the venue until late morning, so there are a lot of people whose names he doesn't know. He promises to try to learn more names. But, he knows this guy, so Cosmo stands and waves back to the G.I.-Joe-looking security guard. "Hi Bob!"

"Ready for doors?" Bob raises his voice to make sure Cosmo can hear him.

"You bet!" Cosmo answers, and sits back down. "I bothered every single production manager and lighting guy

I could meet. Eventually, I got a call from The Cure. If I could be ready to leave that evening, they would give me a shot. That was over thirty years ago. Since then, I've done thousands of shows. Literally, thousands. I'd say it all worked out."

Cosmo has been running shows as a lighting director since 1988, becoming one of the more well-known LDs in the industry. He has worked with Aerosmith, Foreigner, Meatloaf, Mötley Crüe, The Scorpions, The Rolling Stones, and more. Last year, on a long bus ride, he figured out that he's done over seven hundred shows with AC/DC alone.

While he might not be a member of the band or a lyricist, adding a visual element to the concert has truly made Cosmo part of the experience. "The band comes up with the concept. Everyone in the design team adds to that. Absolute consistency is the key to keeping fans happy. The way you heard a song on, say, AC/DC's *Back in Black* album in 1980 is still the way you want to hear that song today, tomorrow, forever. It's what makes a band great. The formula is similar for every album, every show, every tour. Obviously, the lighting has changed over the years due to technology, but I try to stay consistent, like the band. I try to match the sound and keep the experience authentic."

For Cosmo, lighting a show is an art form, and the stage is his canvas. When he listens to music, he can't help but picture the show he'd create for each song. He says it's almost like seeing sound, or hearing color. "Using the AC/DC example, think of 'Rosie.' 'Rosie' is always pink and lavender. 'Shook Me' is always yellow and magenta. 'Dirty Deeds' is done in dirty colors: green and purple, maybe orange. I always use two colors." Cosmo sits up straight, moving his hands to his knees. He is passionate about talking about his passion. "I always use two colors. I like the way it looks. I don't like big saturation on stage unless it's for a specific reason. Like, we might end the show with a big rainbow, but I will only use those color blocks once, because it fits the energy of a finale. I don't share it often, but my very favorite song to light and to listen to is 'Sin City.' It's deep, dark, dirty, evil. There are lavenders, and greens. Dark blues. Heavy guitar. It's just fun. Isn't that the point of all this, to have fun with it?"

The doors must be open. People start trickling in. Slow at first, but soon the audience is entering at a steady stream. Nearly every other person is sporting a band shirt, and some have funny accessories to try to stand out. There are tight jeans, short shorts, and big boots. They are fans, and they have been waiting for this concert for months.

They don't know the crew has already been here for twelve hours. They don't care that this weekend the same show will be in Toronto. All that matters is that somewhere backstage the artists are getting ready. The spirit is contagious. This is how Cosmo preps for the show.

He is happy for the life he leads. "The doors are open. You can literally feel that anticipation in the air." He points toward the public entrance into the arena. "You can't stop loving it. You can't stop getting as excited as them. I love it for all these people streaming in. All the people still waiting outside. Plus"—he smiles—"it helps that I like the music."

CHAPTER FOURTEEN

30 MINUTES UNTIL SHOW TIME

ROAD STORY

"We never had anything growing up. I think my mom only left our county a handful of times, mostly for church. I really didn't expect much as a kid. I figured I'd be working at the factory two towns over, where everyone I graduated with works. I did that for six years, all day. Then I spent all night at the bar. I was not happy. Then, my mom got really sick and had to go to this big city hospital. I went with her, and surprise, surprise, ended up in the bar a lot. One night I started talking to this great group of guys. They all seemed to be really, what's the word? Content. Not just 'drunk, I'm at the bar' kind of happy, like, genuinely pleased with life. I needed to find that. I know now you can't get it all from a job, but it seemed like a good place to start. I took online classes, I volunteered at mom's church and at the high school. Eventually I quit my job and moved to an area where I could start working more shows. I was focused. I was driven toward this, and you know what? I think that's what's made the difference. I'm happier than I've ever been, and not just because I've been to over two dozen different countries by now. It's chasing a project and seeing real results. It sounds lame as hell, but life really is more about the journey."

Lighting Tech, thirty-five years old

MARQUEE

So how does the artist fit into all this?

When real roadies are being real honest about their work, most admit that it doesn't matter who is on stage.

They are quick to explain away the statement.

"Of course it *matters*."

"They sell the tickets."

"They are the reason we all have jobs."

Sure, that's all true. But our jobs aren't driven by fandom. We aren't here to try to make it big (though, the occasional after-party is fun). We aren't here for the celebrity or the spectacle, or to be near someone famous.

We are here to do our jobs. We are here to develop the next generation of gear. We are here to create an experience.

We are part of a team. We are seeing the world. We are adrenaline junkies and musicians. We are carpenters and electricians. We are creatives and technicians.

Every artist is different. Some are friendly, joining the band and crew together as a team. Others trust the system, sticking to their promotion schedules and coming to the venue only to work. Some, of course, are divas dictating policies and, at times, distributing progress. But most just want to do a good job. They want to create an experience for their fans unlike any other.

It is our job to make their vision a functional reality. There is no such thing as 'no,' only 'we'll work it out.' Together these concerts move from city to city, selling out venues and putting on shows.

ARTIST HANDLER

"How did you learn your geography?" Bobby asks. He is responsible for getting the artists: to and from the airport, to and from the hotel, to and from the venue, to and from the stage. We travel in packs. He waits for them, production waits for him, and we keep moving together.

Whoever is performing on stage, whatever kind of performance that is, the artists' job is on that stage. Someone else is taking care of every other step along the way. Stage, lights, mics. Reservations, car rides, interviews, photo shoots, lunch on the go. Someone is planning ahead. Someone is thinking about all the what-ifs. Someone is ready. Here, that someone is Bobby.

Bobby grew up with a few guys who sounded pretty great rapping together. They were friends long before TV spots and world tours. When they started getting popular, they wanted Bobby there. He was "the smart kid," and they trusted him. That trust has kept Bobby employed ever since. From stagehand to stage manager, Bobby fills in where he is needed most. He's "that guy," and every tour needs that guy.

"They let me tag along, so I just figured things out as I went. I remember someone asking me about a kabuki backdrop. I stood there confidently, and straight lied to his face. 'Sure, sure, that works,' then literally ran to look up what I had agreed to. I went to college for sociology, not theatre. But I think well on my feet. I'm a problem solver. My approach as to just be where ever I could be the most helpful, and that changed a lot," says Bobby.

He is currently listed in the tour book as "Artist Handler." Bobby's title makes him laugh. It makes "the artists" laugh, too.

His rich, warm laugh and genuine smile, has a way of infusing any room with a light energy. That's also part of what makes Bobby good at his job. Light brown freckles, a lively head of curls, and a pair of deep dimples make his face uniquely youthful. It is difficult to guess his age, his ethnicity, or what his job might be on the crew. He finds a way to connect with everyone he meets. When Bobby cracks a joke, he holds his tongue between his teeth, just off to the side, and bounces his whole body as he talks. It's easy to understand why people want him around. A professional friend, in a way.

Some people might have trouble with the transition from friend to paid employee, but Bobby embraces it. "It's a circus. Everyone wants to be here, where we are. Look around. We are backstage, with our friends, being paid to put on a show. That's fucking rad. Only a few hundred people in the world ever get to be where we are. How do you want to learn geography? When things get really crazy, I always ask myself that. I'd rather learn it by living it. We've lived geography. We've lived culture, business, all of it. We learned it first-hand on such a huge scale. We know life, because we've experienced it."

The audience is already buzzing. Pictures are being taken. Drinks poured. Everything is larger than life. People crowd toward the stage, trying to catch a glimpse of behind. They don't know what's back there, but they're sure they want to be a part of it. The lines for food, bathrooms and merchandise are long and slow. Some mid-range band has already been on stage, and the crowd is anxious for the headliner. The air is charged. The night is here.

The lighting director, the audio mixing engineer, one audio technician, and two video guys with cameras are in positions at the Front of House. The stage manager and six carpenters are waiting in the wings, stage already set for the first few numbers. The riggers scattered between departments, filling in on spotlight, video, and with some props for the next scene change. Someone from production is waiting with a flashlight by the stairs so no one trips. Everything has been prepped. Everything has been tested. Everyone is in place. It's show time.

It's go time. Bobby's radio reports, "Ready," from each department.

The stage manager has signaled the production manager, "It's a go."

Now the call comes to Bobby.

Is everyone dressed? Has everyone gone to the bathroom? Is security ready to walk? Does everyone have both shoes? Who needs a hat? There is definitely someone who needs their Nicotine gum to make it through the second half. Everyone needs water. Leave the food. Rinse your mouth. Go. Let's go. It's time to go.

"Walking. We are walking," Bobby sends the call through his radio. Everyone is on standby.

Security walks. The artists walk. Bobby walks.

The house lights drop. The dark venue is sprinkled with cell phone lights. Everyone on show crew is in starting positions. Two pats on the back for good luck. Bobby leaves the artist at the edge of the stage. Lights up.

CHAPTER FIFTEEN

ENCORE

THE E.N.D.

We all end our careers on the road in different ways. Some, of course, are lifers. Building shows is what we know, and we won't ever do anything else. Why should we? The road is home, with friends around the world and a warm familiarity with the motion. Most meals are covered and the pay is good. Road pay is definitely a perk. It would be difficult to start a new job and keep a similar income. Stopping would mean a lifestyle change. Maybe there are kids in college, or a mortgage on a house we don't see much, or debts to be paid. Maybe there isn't much at home. Or, simply, because the best nights of sleep come from being tucked into a bus bunk, rolling down the road.

A few of us age out. After years of odd hours, hundreds of thousands of miles, and pushing boxes and pulling cables, our bodies can't help but surrender. Some stop touring because we have to. We can't keep up. Or, our ideas can't keep up. Some are injured at work and are forced to retire. A few aren't invited back. A few seem to evaporate, like we were never there. A few die on the road, and everyone mourns together from around the world.

Some of us choose to leave. We find jobs at theaters or venues, or with the vendors who make the gear. Some leave the industry all together to sell insurance, or run delis. We settle into offices and start families and try our best to embrace a normal life, whatever that means.

Some of us never meant to be roadies. We never meant to build our worlds around rock and roll. We were just trying it out, just having fun. Tour was meant as an experience to try while we were young. Only one tour. Two. Only one more, we swear. Some have been saying that for decades.

I started working for Steve thirteen months into my career and about thirty years into his. He was focused, quiet, and a little odd. He had this goofy way of talking out loud while he worked. We shared an office, but he was hardly ever talking to me directly. Sometimes he'd narrate what he was doing, but most of the time he was talking about history. He would tell elaborate stories tied to whatever region we were playing in, though it always came back to ancient Greece. Steve is Greek, and makes sure everyone knows it.

He was known for his long stories, and sharing an office with him, I heard dozens throughout the day. It had a calming effect, like the hum of the bus generator or a white noise machine that shared moderately interesting historical trivia. He was silly sometimes, making jokes to the mostly empty room. He always wore cowboy boots and called babies aliens. He had two kids, and a wife in Northern California that he talked to at 4:30 p.m., our time, every afternoon.

Steve and I toured together for about two years. Unlike other teams I'd worked with, the two of us worked primarily separate from one another. He had been running shows for years and knew his role well. He didn't want or need anything from me. I was there to do my own job, my own set of tasks. Unless there was a problem to keep me from doing that, he really didn't care. If there was a problem, he always had my back. He was like a weird, nerdy, older-older-brother.

He met my parents once. We were playing Ravinia, a beautiful outdoor amphitheater near where I grew up in Chicago. My mom and dad, one aunt and uncle, and two of my mom's high school friends were coming to see me in action, and of course, hear some "good old rock and roll." My mom had brought her neighborhood-famous butterscotch brownies, separated into three plates: one for the crew, one for the band, and, in a show of true Midwestern hospitality, one to share as she met people backstage. She thought it was wild that rock stars she loved in high school would be eating her treats. My dad was less eager. After years of putting on a suit and tie, working with numbers from nine to five, and coming home to us, he was out of his comfort zone. He didn't understand my emerging career at all. Still, he beamed as I introduced them around to the crew, who were closer to his age than to my own.

Steve liked my parents right away. He sat to talk, eager for the audience. When visitors come around the goal is always to leave them feeling impressed. He had toured with John Denver and Elton John. My mom, of course, loves both. Steve was on fire. When it was time for me to start helping the band get ready for the show, he encouraged them to stay and chat without me. I should do what I had to, and he would keep them entertained.

At the end of the night, after a successful, sold-out show, after my mom yelled, "Freebird!" and the band drove away on their bus, with their brownies, it was time to say goodbye. As I hugged them, they pulled me aside. They were concerned.

Apparently, after I left, the mood grew stern, serious even. Well into his fifties, Steve still had jet black hair to his shoulders. When he had business to take care of, he would swoop the hair behind his ears with both hands. He'd sit on the edge of his desk, trying to look casual. He'd lower his voice, as if sharing a secret.

My parents still quote his speech:

"I like your daughter. She is good at this job. She is smart. She works hard, pays attention to details, though she is often too nice. It is because I like her that I want to tell her she should not be doing this. She still has time to do anything else, and she should. She won't hear it from me. You're her parents; she'll listen to you."

They always laugh at that last part.

Rolling my eyes, I casually shrugged it off, telling my parents not to worry. I packed my stuff like after every show, and crawled onto my own bus to head for another city. I lay in my bunk, telling myself Steve had meant well. Or, my parents had misunderstood his weird sense of humor. Or, that maybe, I'd be fired in the morning.

At the time, I couldn't understand Steve's warning. It hurt my feelings. It felt like I was a child, and he had tattled to my parents. It felt like he wanted me off his team. It felt like I had failed.

I liked my job. At twenty-five, it still felt like a dream. I'd grown to appreciate the long hours and respect the detailed work. I traveled and met all kinds of people and experienced a lot of the world. I was still in awe of the show. I wanted to be there. I wanted to be on that crew list.

In the end, I stepped out quietly. Like I might be back. Like I was just taking a break. I had been slowly and quietly falling in love with a man I'd seen every few months, every few cities. He worked with the staging company. We met at a show, and kept finding ourselves with each other by accident. Then, we started seeing each other on purpose. One day he asked if I'd go with him on his next big adventure. We'd move somewhere new. We'd find a house—one we'd live in, together, more often than not. It would be a home that would lead to a dog and some kids and a life off the road. I didn't realize it was the end. There was always the idea that I would go back out on tour, when it was time. Maybe in a few months, or next year. Maybe never.

I understand Steve's speech differently now.

This industry, in its beauty, weirdness and splendor, is perpetual. Through wars and recessions and technical evolution and all of human history, people have wanted to be entertained. From storytellers to movie directors, authors to show designers, audiences are looking for a something to carry them away. Generation after generation, artisans have adapted ways to provide those moments. The show goes on.

But that means, there will always be another show. Another long show day. Another tour. The next tour needs to be bigger and bolder and heavier and more complex than the last. It wasn't that long ago that concerts were just instruments. Then, instruments, audio, and lights. Now, there are small cities of people and gear going on tour for months at a time.

There is a proverb, of sorts, in show business: "You are only as good as your last gig." That kind of hustle can be exhausting, and things are only speeding up. There is always a new piece of technology, a new production manager, a new artist. There is no guessing what things might look like in another ten years.

But there is also a freedom in the motion. Specifics to each gig, each show, each moment will change, but another is waiting. A new idea. A new innovation. A new generation of young hopefuls ready to make their mark.

Artists and technicians and musicians and mechanics all working together toward the moment when, in the dark before a show, the air is electric, the stakes immediate, and the audience is there waiting.

ACKNOWLEDGMENTS

Many people have helped in the vision for this book. Not only the individuals portrayed as characters, but also the dozens of people who contributed their expertise, their support, and time out of their busy show day schedules to teach me about their world. I feel privileged to be able to tell this story. Thank you.

However, without a few very key people, this book would not be a reality. In no particular order, a big YOU'RE THE BEST to the following rock stars:

Matthew Hales, Harper Hales, Holden Hales, Huxley Hales, The Pfennig Pfamily, The Hales Family, Our Chewelah Family, The Levine Family, The White Family; Elizabeth Curto, Steve Voudouris, Tom Fischer, Tim Miller, Andrea Shirk, Suzi Meyer, Troy Clair, Adam Davis, Steve Moles, Colin O'Flaherty; Ben Bickel, Gary Ferenchak, Bobby Grant, Bryan Humphries, John Ogle, Greg Price, Dale "Opie" Skjerseth, Jason "Attaboy" Statler, Madison Wade, Cosmo Wilson; Philip Gerard, Maddy Blais, Jacob Levenson, Suzannah Lessard, Leslie Rubinkowski, all my fellow Gophers at Goucher College, MFA in Creative Nonfiction; Steve Timm, Larry Abed, Greg Shwipps, Donna Messina, Don McLaughlin, Memsy Price, and Keidi Keating

Lightning Source UK Ltd.
Milton Keynes UK
UKHW022330070622
404086UK00005BC/219